The Girl in the Green Raincoat

BY LAURA LIPPMAN

The Girl in the Green Raincoat

I'd Know You Anywhere

Life Sentences

Hardly Knew Her

Another Thing to Fall

What the Dead Know

No Good Deeds

To the Power of Three

By A Spider's Thread

Every Secret Thing

The Last Place

In a Strange City

The Sugar House

In Big Trouble

Butchers Hill

Charm City

Baltimore Blues

The Girl in the Green Raincoat

Laura Lippman

This book is a work of fiction. References to real people, events, establishments, organizations, or locales are intended only to provide a sense of authenticity, and are used fictitiously. All other characters, and all incidents and dialogue, are drawn from the author's imagination and are not to be construed as real.

Originally published by *The New York Times Magazine*.

HarperCollins books may be purchased for educational, business, or sales promotional use. For information please write: Special Markets Department, HarperCollins Publishers, 10 East 53rd Street, New York, NY 10022.

FIRST HARPERLUXE EDITION

HarperLuxe™ is a trademark of HarperCollins Publishers

Library of Congress Cataloging-in-Publication Data is available upon request.

ISBN: 978-0-06-193856-6

11 12 13 14 ID/RRD 10 9 8 7 6 5 4 3 2 1

For Niki, Claire, Logan, and Nash

Chapter 1

"I am being held hostage," Tess Monaghan whispered into her iPhone. "By a terrorist. The agenda is unclear, the demands vague, but she's prepared to hold me here for at least two months. Twelve weeks or eighteen years, depending on how you look at it."

"Nice way to talk about our future child," said her boyfriend, Crow, tucking a quilt around her, although it was a typical early autumn Baltimore, not at all chilly. The quilt was a gift from Crow's mother, an artist with an exceptional eye, which made up for her lapses when it came to the nickname she had allowed her only son to keep into adulthood. Under normal circumstances Tess would have been thrilled by this updated version of a Geese-in-Flight, rendered in her favorite colors: muted greens and golds chosen to complement the recently winterized sun porch. But it was another reminder of her captivity, no different from an orange jumpsuit.

All summer long she had looked forward to sitting in this addition to her bungalow, watching the leaves change, warming her back at the two-faced fireplace connected to the living room. But that anticipation had been based on her belief that she would be able to leave the room when she wanted, not forced to lie here for days on end, under strict instructions to move as little as possible. Much to her horror, there had even been a discussion of bedpans, and her well-intentioned aunt had sent her an antique chamber pot. The doctor told Tess she could avoid that indignity, except perhaps at night. "As long as you don't overdo it," she added. Overdo a slow waddle to the bathroom! This made no sense to Tess. Raucous fun could be overdone. Drinking could be overdone. High-fat food could be overdone, even exercise. But a ten-foot walk to the bathroom?

"Bring wine," she hissed into the phone. "And Matthew's pizza. Those lima beans with feta cheese from Mezze. Sopapillas from Golden West. Hurry!"

Crow took the phone from her gently. Oh, he was forever gentle, wasn't he, except when his sperm was storming the gates of one's diaphragm, eluding spermicide and wiggling its way into the winner's circle, a 99-to-1 long shot that drilled into her unsuspecting egg, creating the truculent would-be person who now had her pinned to this wicker chaise longue.

"You're welcome to visit," he told her oldest and best friend, Whitney Talbot. "And she's actually allowed to have some salt, within normal limits. She's joking about the wine."

"I am not! If this state weren't so backward, I could buy wine on the Internet. Stupid protectionist liquor lobby. I bet Eddie's will deliver, if it comes to that."

"They probably would," Crow agreed, bidding Whitney goodbye and placing the iPhone on the stack of books that Tess's aunt had sent with the chamber pot, trying to anticipate all her moods and whims. "But I've already spoken to them about our situation and your dietary requirements for the next ten weeks. Meanwhile, watch your tone. Even mock outrage can goose your blood pressure. In fact—"

He took the cuff out. Tess already hated the sight of it. "Most expensive bracelet I've ever owned," she muttered as he fitted it over her left bicep, and although the device was only eighty-nine dollars, this was a literal truth. That eighty-nine dollars was the first of many expenses, she now realized, that would not be covered by the modest "group health insurance" she had set up for her company. She would need a family plan, which cost four times as much, and even then there might be more unanticipated expenses that could drain their savings. She willed herself to calm down as the cuff swelled and deflated. But being angry was preferable to being scared, and she had been extremely scared since ending up in the E.R. three days ago.

The first warning bell, in hindsight, had been the ease with which she'd sat through five hours of surveillance without a twinge of discomfort. Normally, the ability to last hours before her bladder asserting herself would be a cause for celebration in Tess Monaghan's world. Although many manufacturers had tried, there was no perfect solution for what she called the feminine relief problem. Men had more options, especially if they weren't shy. Since becoming a private investigator six years ago, she had trained herself to be extremely stoic, and often blessed her father for those early years, when his insistence on making good time on family trips taught a young Tess to sync her body to the family's ancient station wagon's need for fuel. Edging into her third trimester, she discovered that pregnancy inevitably took its toll on her stalwart bladder, making surveillance problematic. Which was a problem, for surveillance was the bread-and-butter mainstay of Keys Investigations. That and Dumpster-diving, which she had reluctantly put on hold since she learned she was pregnant.

However, pregnancy turned out to be an excellent cover for surveillance. Women looked at her belly, not her face. Men looked away from her. Especially the one man she was determined to catch on her iPhone's camera, a deadbeat dad named Jordan Baum. A house painter, he maintained via his attorney that he had taken a bad fall on a job, sustaining the impossible-to-disprove "soft tissue damage." His baby mama believed that Jordan was a cheater twice over, working off the books for a contractor who preferred to pay in cash, allowing Jordan to shortchange her and the government.

But Jordan Baum was cagey enough not to take jobs that placed him in public view. Over the week that Tess had been watching him, he'd hobbled in and out of a major rehab near the Canton waterfront, and while it was suspicious for an out-of-work painter to keep visiting a house-under-renovation, it wasn't proof of anything. Stymied, she arranged for an attractive blonde to cross his path, a blonde who would prove much unluckier to Jordan Baum than any black cat.

On the appointed day, Whitney hid around the corner from the work site until alerted by text message that Jordan was making his faux laborious way toward the building. Whitney sailed out, arms piled high with stacks of paper. Tess had asked only that she drop them, but Whitney literally threw herself into the role, sprawling at Jordan's feet, screaming in horror as her papers scattered, faking an injury to her knee. Gallant Jordan ran about—sometimes limping, sometimes not—gathered the papers, and helped Whitney to her feet. She insisted on buying him coffee at a nearby diner. All the while, Tess was snapping photos of the miraculously healed Jordan. These would be enough to make him kick in what he owed his ex. The IRS could hire its own private investigator to get their piece.

"But once a cheater, always a cheater," Tess told Whitney over a celebratory late lunch at Matthew's Pizza. "He'll pay for a while, then fall behind again. Without a regular check to garnish, it's impossible to make him stay current."

"Did you know he has four kids by three different women?" Whitney asked. "He actually took their photos out of his wallet and said, 'I make beautiful babies.' Is that a new seduction technique, advertising one's bona fides as a baby daddy? I mean, I know I lead a relatively sheltered life, but—what's wrong, Tess?"

Tess had finally registered the strange absence of her bladder's demands. The realization was quickly followed by a pressing *presence*—intense cramps, then a stretch of violent vomiting, first in the restaurant's tiny ladies' room, then on the sidewalk, then the gutter, and finally down the side of Whitney's Suburban as Whitney rushed her to Johns Hopkins. "It's seen worse," Whitney said when Tess apologized between retching episodes. "My mom's corgis are prone to diarrhea."

The tale unspooled in the E.R., where the doctors tended to Tess with reassuringly brisk confidence. Preeclampsia was just another day at the office for them. At thirty-five, Tess was officially a high-risk pregnancy. She was at risk, her child was at risk, and unless she wanted to deliver a baby the size of a bratwurst—Whitney had provided that elegant image—she must spend the rest of her pregnancy in bed.

"Remember how you used to say you would love to take time off just to read and watch movies?" Crow asked her now, continuing to bustle around the room, putting a vase of flowers on the mantel, then moving them to the windowsill. For a straight man, he was alarmingly in touch with his inner Martha Stewart. He seemed to have inherited the nesting phase that would normally be Tess's, but that was true even before her diagnosis. He had wanted to paint the baby's room, throw a shower. Tess, falling back on the traditions of her mother's Jewish family, insisted it was bad luck.

"I used to say a lot of things." Interestingly, she had never said she wanted to be a mother, but she did not remind Crow of this. His joy at the news had been unadulterated. If he ever had any fears or doubts about fatherhood, she never saw them. Crow, reliable as sunrise, was not one of the Jordan Baums of the world—right? She had not planned to be a mother, but she had not planned *not* to be a mother. Her whole life was governed by accidents—her career, her relationship, even this house that she so loved. It made sense that her future daughter would continue this pattern.

And if her daughter turned out to be a precocious pain in the butt in the bargain—well, she knew whose DNA that was, too.

Crow said: "With Mrs. Blossom now working for you full-time, you can afford to take the time away from the office. You were comfortable with her taking over during your maternity leave. What's an extra two months?"

"Two months of reduced billings. Prodigy though Mrs. Blossom may be, she's only one woman."

"One woman ran your business for years," Crow said. "Everything will be all right.

"You don't *know* that."

"No one knows anything, in the end."

Those words could be a comfort or a curse. For once, Tess decided to accept the comfort. The sun was beginning to set, and although her porch faced east, she could see the effect in the amber light that filtered through the still-green leaves. The porch was cantilevered out from the house, which was built into the side of a steep, wooded hill, so it felt like a tree house. *Rock-a-bye, Tess, in the treetops.* Surrounded by books and Crow's towering stack of Criterion Collection DVDs, she could improve her mind while her body held her here. She could read the great books, study maps of the world, attack the ideas—philosophy, economics—she had bypassed in college.

Or she could stare wistfully out the window, into the park, where the local dog walkers were beginning to file in. A week ago she had been among them, exercising her greyhound and Doberman, Esskay and Miata. How she missed that, she thought, forgetting all the times she had complained about the chore, how often she'd yearned to sleep in while the greyhound bathed her with hot, fishy breath. (Part of the reason she was on the sun porch was that Esskay would not fight her for the chaise longue, the way she did for the queen bed in the master bedroom.) Yes, she had longed for time off, for a chance to read more, to be absolved from the morning walks that fell to her. But she had imagined herself *on* a beach, not shaped like a beach ball.

Her eye was drawn to a miniature version of Esskay, a prancing greyhound, a true gray one, whereas Esskay was black with a patch of white at her breast. The little dog wore a green jacket belted around its middle and moved with the cocky self-confidence of someone used to being noticed. As did its human companion, in a tightly cinched celery-green raincoat that was a twin to the greyhound's. Hard to tell the woman's age at this distance, but Tess could make out sleek blond hair, a wasp-waisted figure. She was the kind of pretty-pretty woman who would be called a girl into her forties. She ignored the other dog owners, cradling what appeared to be a cell phone against her ear. Tess frowned. She believed that dog owners, like their dogs, should experience the walk on a Zen level of being. She wished she could see the woman more clearly, make out the expression on her face.

"Is there anything else you need to make your haven perfect?" Crow asked.

"Binoculars," Tess said.

That had been Sunday; she had the binoculars by Monday. And for the rest of the week, Tess did, in fact, read quite a bit and began to catch up with the films that Crow thought essential to cultural literacy. But each afternoon, she picked up her new binoculars and watched the dogs converge on the park, then studied the girl in the green raincoat as she stalked past them, her prancing little greyhound leading the way. The girl was always on the phone, it seemed, but perhaps she was shy and using that as a cover. The dog walkers of Stony Run could be a cliquey bunch. Even seen through high-powered binoculars, the woman's face betrayed little emotion. Her walks lasted longer than most; at least she was giving her high-strung dog plenty of exercise. Monday, Tuesday, Wednesday, Thursday, the pattern was the same. Only the footwear changed, her chic version of Wellies switched out for brown suede boots as the ground dried. *Still, so impractical,* Tess thought, watching Friday afternoon as the girl in the green raincoat glided into the park. Didn't her dog ever leap up, leave muddy paw prints?

"You're getting weird," Crow said, bringing in her supper tray, their own dogs following like troubled handmaidens. They were upset by Tess's displacement from the master bedroom, even if Esskay did enjoy having more of the bed. But Esskay seemed to sense a bigger change was coming, and she wasn't sure she liked it.

Join the club, sister.

Tess had abandoned her binoculars and begun to eat her supper when she noticed Esskay, a sight hound at heart, perk up her ears and run to the window. Probably a squirrel or even a leaf. The sight hound's sight wasn't particularly reliable.

But what had drawn Esskay's eye, in this instance, was her own tiny doppelganger, running through the park. Running through the park, quite alone, celery-green leash lashing. Running like a thing pursued, except—it wasn't. For no matter how long Tess watched that evening—and she kept her vigil well into the night, turning out her lights the better to see into the gloom—the girl in the green raincoat never reappeared.

Chapter 2

"If you're going to play *Rear Window*, then I think Crow needs to swan around in a green peignoir set," Whitney said the next day, as Tess continued her vigil on the sun porch. Neither girl nor dog had shown up for their usual sunset walk.

"I thought you for Grace Kelly, bony WASP that you are," Tess said, frowning at the supper that Crow had fixed. It was perfectly healthy—a spinach salad, risotto made with shiitake mushrooms and butternut squash from the farmer's market. It was delicious, too. But the lack of choice, the closing off of options, made her crazy. Occasionally she liked to have a Goldenberg Peanut Chew for lunch, or a bag of Utz crab chips.

"The Talbots and the Kellys are distantly related," Whitney said. It was plausible, although with

Whitney's sharp jaw and athletic posture, the Kelly she most resembled was Jack, the rower for whom Kelly Drive in Philadelphia was named. Both Whitney and Tess had rowed in college, but Whitney had been better. That was pretty much the story of their long friendship—whatever they did, Whitney was better. Whitney got better grades. Whitney was faster, a more competitive rower who had transferred to Yale and been the stroke on a women's lightweight four. She excelled in the newspaper business, too, a field where Tess had failed. Whitney then chucked it all to work at her family's foundation. Because, yes, on top of everything else, she was rich, someone who had never known a single care about money. Whitney Talbot excelled at everything—except relationships. She lived in a guest cottage on the grounds of her parents' house out in the valley and proclaimed herself a spinster. It was easier than admitting she was lonely, Tess suspected.

"I'm so clearly the Thelma Ritter in this scenario," Whitney said now. "Only taller. Remember the first time you see Grace Kelly in *Rear Window*, popping into the frame as Jimmy Stewart awakes from his nap. She was so beautiful I literally gasped."

"I remember it more as an asthmatic wheeze, in which your knees jerked up, spilling a tub of buttered popcorn all over the man in front of you."

"No, that was a horror film," Whitney said. "*Aliens*? *Reanimator*? We were at the Charles, back in the day when it was one big theater, and we would go to late movies, then to the Club Charles and drink until two A.M." She addressed Tess's stomach. "I knew your mother when she was *fun*, you little parasite."

Tess frowned, and Whitney, in a rare burst of sensitivity, recognized she had overstepped. "Have you thought about names?"

"Not really," Tess lied. She and Crow had learned quickly this was dangerous territory. "We're going to honor the Jewish tradition of choosing the name of someone no longer alive. Actually, we're going whole hog on the Jewish traditions. No baby shower, no fixing up the room ahead of time. Don't want the evil eye to fasten its gaze on us."

Her tone was light, self-mocking, but Whitney wasn't fooled. "It will be okay, Tess."

Tess tried to make a casual motion of assent, part shrug and wave. Unfortunately, she had a forkful of risotto halfway to her mouth and succeeded only in flinging it at the window.

"Postcard from your future," Whitney said, removing the clump of rice and dividing it between the two dogs, vigilant sentries whenever food was consumed.

"Why hasn't she come back?" Tess fretted, incapable of keeping her eyes away from the park, much less keeping her mind from this topic.

"If the dog ran away, she doesn't have a dog to walk."

"But she would have come through, looking for the dog, right? And if the dog ended up running home, as Crow insists, then they would be out walking again, right? Something happened, Whitney. Has there been anything on the news about a missing woman, about some strange incident in North Baltimore?"

"For the tenth time—no, Tess."

"I haven't asked you ten times."

"But you've been bugging Crow all day. He told me. Read a book." Whitney looked through the stack. "Your Aunt Kitty's as eclectic as ever, I see. The only commonality I divine here is that most of the books are big and fat."

"Like me," Tess said, bitter at her body's betrayal. It wasn't just her blood pressure and the baby mound that seemed designed to give her permanent indigestion. Her feet were so swollen she couldn't wear anything but slippers or an old pair of Uggs, and she fit into those only after Crow sliced open the seams.

"Here's a skinny one—*The Daughter of Time*, by Josephine Tey."

"A comfort read, I've read it a dozen times." And, like its main character, she was determined to solve a mystery from her sickbed. "Look, why can't you and Crow just go around, canvass the neighborhood, see if anyone knows the dog or the woman?"

"Tess—"

"I'm worried," she said, putting on a pout, although she knew she didn't do it well. "When I worry, my blood pressure starts to rise."

Whitney wasn't fooled, Tess could tell that much. But she was a loyal person, one inclined to indulge the whims of a confined friend.

"We'll do that tomorrow," Whitney said. "It's Sunday, people will be home. Maybe we'll find 'missing' posters for the dog, which would ease your mind. But, really, Tess, why can't you become obsessed with online poker or Scrabulous, like a normal person?"

"As if you would be friends with a normal person."

True to Whitney's word, Whitney and Crow set off the next afternoon to see if anyone in the neighborhood had lost an Italian greyhound. It was the kind of late fall day that Whitney loved—not crisp and golden. That was predictable, banal. No, this day was overcast, with the scent of fires in the air, the leaves beginning to thin. Winter was coming, and Whitney liked winter, along with its attendant sports, although it was rare now to have a cold snap long enough to freeze the stock pond where she had learned to skate. Last year had been completely snow-free, without a single day to go cross-country skiing. Whitney had a well-trained mind and she knew her anecdotal experiences were proof of nothing, but she believed in climate change and worried that things might be far more dire than anyone realized. How did someone bring a child onto this fragile planet, when it might not even exist in a few decades? She could not decide if Tess was incredibly brave or incredibly stupid.

Of course, some people do go both ways, as the scarecrow liked to say.

Crow said: "I thought we would start about three blocks north of here, working up Woodlawn, down Hawthorne, then up Keswick, going to every other house, doing evens up and odds down."

"Why every other?"

"People are going to know if they have a neighbor on the block with a miniature greyhound. We'll cover more houses this way."

"We'd cover more still if we split up."

"I considered that," Crow said. "But you know what, Whitney? We never talk, you and me. It's never just the two of us."

"True." *And that's the natural order of things,* Whitney wanted to say. She liked Crow, approved of him as Tess's partner. She was always happy to be in the company of both. But Crow wasn't her friend, he was her friend's . . . boyfriend? Baby daddy? God, she hoped they would get married, if only to simplify the issue of nomenclature.

"Besides I have something kind of serious I want to talk to you about."

Whitney thought that the primary advantage of not being in a relationship was never hearing those dreaded words. "Let's start here," she said. "On this block of Hawthorne."

They threaded their way through some of the nicer blocks of Roland Park, very nice blocks indeed. This, Whitney thought, was the model that the suburbs should imitate. The houses were large, but not overly so, and there was a careless, rambling quality to many of them, as if they had grown over the years to accommodate growing families. Most were shingled, a maintenance headache to be sure, but they blended with the landscape instead of fighting it. A Sunday afternoon walk in Roland Park, with glimpses into foyers where boots and shoes were lined up at the foot of gleaming oak stairs, could almost make one yearn for a family. Almost.

But of those people they found at home, no one knew of a greyhound and its green-coated owner. It was almost five and the light was fading when they began moving south.

"Executive decision," Crow said. "Let's amend Tess's plan and work toward the business district, where people are more likely to post signs for missing dogs."

Whitney hadn't realized that Crow ever ignored Tess's orders. She liked him better for it. "Let's."

The houses here were smaller, the places where the workers had lived while building the grander homes of Roland Park. At a modest duplex on Schenley Road, a harried-looking woman opened her door a crack, just enough for Whitney to see a house in chaos, with three small children running around in the small living room, not one of them fully clothed.

"You're looking for a greyhound?" she repeated. "A little one? Wait here."

Within minutes she was back at the door with a dog that fit Tess's description—silvery gray, green collar and leash still attached. The coat was clearly custom-made. Doggie couture, how decadent. Whitney's family might have been wealthy, but they weren't given to *flash*.

"I found this one rooting in my garbage yesterday. I was going to advertise, but you can take her, seeing as how you know who the owner is and all."

"We don't—" Crow began.

"You take her," the woman repeated, placing the dog in Crow's arms, where it writhed and snapped. "My children wanted to keep her, but I know that's not right, even if she doesn't have a tag on that fancy collar, or an ID on the little coat. You take her. 'Bye!"

"No, Mommy!" a girl's voice shrieked. "Don't give Scooby away!" Other voices joined in and the scene quickly escalated to a three-ring tantrum, with children throwing their bodies around the living room in heaving despair.

"Please," the woman hissed, "take the dog."

Whitney thought she heard the woman mutter "And God help you." The poor thing definitely seemed overwhelmed. But surely that was because of her children?

"Mission accomplished!" she said to Crow. "What was it you wanted to talk about?"

"Maybe later," he said, with a backward glance at the house. The children's piteous screams were still quite audible. "Let's go settle the matter of Tess's 'satiable curiosity."

"She's always been a little like the elephant in Kipling," Whitney conceded. "And now she sort of looks like him."

"Well, it's clear why the dog was abandoned," Crow said a day later as he cleaned up yet another mess made by the Italian greyhound. Esskay and Miata looked on in disgust.

"Abandonment is one theory," Tess said. "But let's not rule out the possibility that this dog killed her owner and buried the body in the park."

In the twenty-four hours since they took possession of the greyhound, it had: relieved itself in the house six times, attempted to steal food from Esskay and Miata, chewed on one of Tess's Uggs, and all but consumed the paperback of *The Daughter of Time.* It had also snarled at Crow and tried to bite him when he attempted to separate the dog from the Ugg. They had borrowed a crate from a neighbor, but getting the dog into the crate was no small feat, and once in, he would soil it, flying in the face of everything Tess thought she knew about dogs.

"A rescue group might be able to put us in touch with local breeders, and breeders could tell us if they've recently placed a dog in the area," Crow said as he abandoned all pretense of luring the dog into the crate and muscled him in, only to have it nip at his arms and face. "It's worth a try."

"So is exorcism," Tess said.

Even as she spoke, her well-trained thumbs had found a local rescue group for Italian greyhounds on her iPhone's Web connection and a single tap dialed the phone number. The rescue group coordinator gave her a list of East Coast breeders, while warning darkly that this problem child sounded like the work of someone unscrupulous, a puppy mill that wouldn't be among her contacts. But after four phone calls—and four earnest lectures on the special needs of Italian greyhounds and how different they were from their larger racing cousins—Tess found an upstate New York breeder who had placed a dog in Baltimore several weeks ago.

"It was a sweet dog," he insisted, "normal as pie." He gave Tess the name and number of a local man who lived on Blythewood Road, which lay east of the park and therefore just outside Tess's search grid. It was a grand street, one of the nicest in all of North Baltimore, the kind of place where dogs might wear designer raincoats. She was pleased at how neatly everything was falling into place. Perhaps she could do her job from bed after all.

"May I speak to Don Epstein?" Tess asked when a man answered the phone.

"You got him."

"My name is Tess Monaghan and we have what I believe is your dog, a miniature greyhound who was found on Schenley Avenue just two days ago."

"Really?"

His response struck Tess as odd. He seemed surprised, yet suspicious, too. Shouldn't he know his dog was missing? Shouldn't he care?

"Yes, and my boyfriend would be happy to bring it back to you—"

"No, thanks."

Now it was Tess's turn to be surprised. And suspicious. "But—"

"Look, I'll give you a reward for your time and effort. But I don't want that dog. It's hell on wheels. I think the breeder lied through his teeth when he unloaded that monster on me."

Yet the rescue group coordinator had told her that this particular breeder had a stellar reputation.

"What about your"—she took a guess—"wife?"

"What about her?" Brusque, curt.

"She's the one I saw walking the dog, down in the park. I assume it's her dog?"

"Yeah, well, she won't miss it, either. I'll put a check in the mail, but don't even think of bringing that dog back here. I want nothing to do with it."

He hung up. Without, Tess couldn't help noticing, taking down details that would allow him to make good on the offer of a check. A deadbeat doggie dad. A first for her, but she didn't see how it would be that different from making the more common kind live up to his responsibilities.

Chapter 3

Mr. Epstein?"

The woman who stood on the front steps of Don Epstein's home looked ridiculous. She should. She worked hard enough at it. She wore a fuchsia trench coat, unbuttoned to reveal the riotous flower print of her dress, flower prints being an unavoidable signature look for a woman named Mrs. Blossom. Her shoes were hot pink, high-top Reeboks, circa 1985. She had unearthed a cache of these lumpy wonders at a flea market, a virtual Reebok rainbow—pink, orange, red, yellow, white. She cared for her Reeboks as if they were custom-made Italian pumps, massaging them with special cream, buffing the toes, even stuffing them with tissue paper at night. The shoes might not flatter her sturdy calves, but they were kind to her feet. And as the late Mr. Blossom liked to say: "Without your feet, where would you stand on anything?"

Besides, Don Epstein wouldn't be the first person to dismiss Felicia Blossom on a glance. Tess Monaghan herself had thought Mrs. Blossom a bit dull when they first met, and now Mrs. Blossom was bucking for an equity share in Keys Investigations. She was sorry, of course, for the reason behind this opportunity. After all, that child was going to be Mrs. Blossom's almost grandbaby, her consolation prize for living so far from her biological grandchildren, now in Arizona. But she was glad for the chance to show Tess the range and breadth of her talents.

"Whatever you're selling, we're not interested," her quarry said. He might have slammed the door if Mrs. Blossom had not planted one pink, padded foot on the threshold.

"I'm from BARCs, the city animal shelter." She flashed a business card, designed and printed by Crow a mere hour ago. "We want to discuss your fiduciary responsibilities for the dog you abandoned."

Tess had argued that *fiduciary* was too grandiose, perhaps inaccurate, but Mrs. Blossom decided it was just right for a self-important civil servant. In fact, she had approached this whole venture as a Method actor might, thinking long and hard about her "character."

Her alter ego lived in Northeast Baltimore, in one of those small but charming bungalows. She had seven grandchildren. Her husband was on disability; the household needed her paycheck.

"Excuse me?"

"As costs rise and public funding falls, we've taken a page out of the Department of Social Services playbook and decided to seek renumeration from pet parents who dump their offspring into the system. That's the only way we can avoid resorting to almost immediate euthanasia."

"Kill the mutt," Epstein said. "I don't care."

Don Epstein was playing out their scene exactly as Tess had envisioned, but it was dismaying nonetheless. Mrs. Blossom produced the jargon-laded "authorization form"—again, Tess's idea, Crow's execution—and indicated where he was to sign. He scrawled his name, not even bothering to read the presumptive death warrant.

"And, of course, we'll need your wife's signature," she said, pointing to a second line.

"My wife's?"

"The people who brought us the dog supplied the breeder's name, which is how we found you. He says you both signed the contract. Therefore, we need two signatures to proceed."

He was the kind of man who flushed when angry—not red, but a deep, eggplant purple. It would be a nice shade on a shoe, come to think of it, but it didn't flatter a face. Don Epstein, with his dark hair and heavy beard, looked a little like a werewolf. Mr. Blossom, rest his soul, had been as sweet as the surname he had bestowed on her more than fifty years ago.

"You can force me to pay for this mutt's care, but I don't have the authority to waive custody? That's insane."

"All I need is your wife's signature—"

"She's not here."

Tess had anticipated this answer, too.

"Has she left for work? I can always visit her office."

"My wife is, um, self-employed."

"So she's—"

"Gone. On a business trip."

"When do you expect her back?"

"I don't. That is, I don't know. She's a, uh, free spirit. Comes and goes as she pleases."

"Where did she go?"

"That's none of your business."

He slammed the door. A heavy wooden affair, perhaps it couldn't help closing with such thudding finality. Mrs. Blossom didn't know architecture, but the house suggested "Italian" to her, with its sand-colored stucco walls and red tiled roof. It sprawled over an enormous lawn, presumably tended by landscaping crews. Not to stereotype—after all, that's what people were forever doing to her—but Mr. Epstein looked too blow-dried to be the gardening type. He had a fresh manicure and two gleaming rings. She would jot those details down later. Funny, her memory, which had been growing unreliable, was sharpening since she took this job. *Tight, shiny maroon shirt*, she added to her mental inventory. *A gold bracelet, too, ID style.*

His taste in houses was better than his taste in jewelry. Even in today's deflated market, this was a million-dollar home or better, and a million dollars bought a lot of house in Baltimore city.

Instead of walking down the flagstone path to where her car sat at the curb, she wandered toward the garage as if confused. Confusion was an older woman's prerogative, after all. The garage had small diamond-pane windows that allowed her to peer in. A three-car garage, it held only two vehicles—a BMW SUV and a low-slung Porsche that made her back hurt just looking at it. Imagine getting in and out of such a car. Mr. Epstein was only in his fifties, by her estimation, but he was a big man. She tried to memorize the license plates, a much trickier task. Luckily, one was a vanity tag, although she couldn't sort out its meaning: MLCRISS.

"Mid-life crisis!" Tess hooted. "Interesting thing to announce to the world. But where's the trophy wife that usually comes with the package?"

"She's on a business trip," Mrs. Blossom said.

"He *says*," Tess scoffed. "What else did you get from your background checks?"

Mrs. Blossom read from her notes: "He owns a chain of check-cashing businesses, with five franchises in Baltimore alone."

"Some of those guys are legit, but I bet he's one of the scummy ones, preying on welfare recipients, making payday loans at exorbitant interest rates. How long has he been married?"

"Six months ago, according to the license. First marriage for her—Carole Massinger Epstein—but not for him. License says he was widowed."

"Newspaper searches?"

"Not much, but then—the *Beacon-Light* database online only goes back to 1995. He pops up in some stories about check-cashing owners worried about electronic benefits, and that's that."

"And Carole?"

"She's younger, thirty-two to his fifty-three. But that's all I've been able to find so far."

"What about the MVA?"

"The two cars I saw are registered to him, although at an old address in Anne Arundel County. So he doesn't update things, timely. But her car is newer, bought only three months ago, so it carries the Blythewood address. A BMW convertible, green, according to the registration."

"So, if Mr. Epstein is to be believed," Tess said, "his wife got into her spanking new BMW, drove off on a business trip, and never mentioned that she lost their new dog. Who would do that?"

"The dog is a bit of a . . . handful."

"He's not *that* bad," Tess said. The still nameless dog had stopped soiling the crate, although he was still inclined to snap and snarl at almost everyone. With the exception of Tess, whom he seemed to regard as a fellow captive in a most unusual jail. If only he could speak, they might enjoy one of those terrific bonding experiences common to prison movies. *The Dog in the Iron Crate, The Kiss of the Greyhound, The Preeclampsia Redemption.*

Mrs. Blossom eyed the crate warily. "You know, I met Mr. Blossom because of a dog. Did I ever tell you that?"

"No," Tess said. "I know you married him less than a month after your first date, but you've never mentioned the circumstances."

"I was at the bus stop. I was a student at Notre Dame College, and I honestly thought I might become a nun. I didn't want to be a nun, but boys didn't like me much. I had a nice figure, and my skin was clear, but I didn't know how to talk to boys, so I thought, *I'll be a nun, and then people won't notice I don't have boyfriend.*" She looked embarrassed by this admission. "I was only seventeen."

"You don't have to be seventeen to think that way," Tess assured her.

"Anyway, I was at the bus stop on Charles Street. And this stray dog tried to cross the street, which was about the busiest street in Baltimore before all the highways came through. I didn't think, I just ran into the street after it. This one man, he threw on his brakes, but the man behind him didn't react fast enough and he hit the man in front of him. And that man was so angry, and he got out of his car and the two drivers started yelling at each other, then yelling at me—"

"And the man who braked, that was Mr. Blossom?"

"No, no."

"The man who hit him?"

"*No*, not him, either. Mr. Blossom was standing on the other side of the street, waiting for the northbound bus."

"What does that have to do with the dog or the accident?"

"I got so flustered, I ran to the other side of the street. This nice young man—I didn't know his name yet—said to me, 'Why don't you just stay here for a minute or two, and let those two gentlemen work out their problem?' So I did and the next thing I knew, his bus had come and gone, and my bus had come and gone, and we walked down to Cold Spring, where there used to be an old-fashioned soda fountain, and we talked and we talked and, well, we never really stopped."

"Really? You were married for more than fifty years and you never ran out of things to say to each other?"

"Oh, we learned to be quiet with each other, too. But it was always a good quiet. We were never cross with each other."

"Never?" That seemed unfathomable to Tess. Crow was the most easygoing man in the world, and he drove her to distraction several times a week. A long marriage, raising children with someone—it simply wasn't possible not to get angry or irritable at times. "How did you manage that?"

"Whenever I got cross with him, I would think about that girl at the bus stop, how unhappy she was, how she thought no one could ever want to take her on a date, much less love her. It may sound silly, but

I figured out that being happy made me happier than being unhappy ever did."

Tess replayed these words in her head: *Being happy made me happier than being unhappy.* The statement was so nonsensical it was profound.

"Do you realize," she said, "that your romance with Mr. Blossom was literally a shaggy dog story?"

Mrs. Blossom looked confused. "But that dog wasn't shaggy at all. He was a terrier, clipped very close."

"I meant—oh, never mind. Thanks for all your help today."

Left alone with her laptop, Tess glanced out the window at Stony Run Park and sighed. Technology had come so far, so quickly, but it wasn't far enough. Here, with her laptop balanced on an old-fashioned wicker breakfast tray, she could roam the Internet, finding information that once took hours, even days. Here was the assessment and purchase information on Don Epstein's Blythewood home, and the old addresses on his vehicle registration allowed her to look up his previous house, which had been even more expensive, a $4 million house on Gibson Island. But even as her wireless connection allowed her to collapse time and space, it could never provide the *serendipity* of legwork she had known—first as a reporter, roaming the hallways of courthouses and government buildings, then as an investigator. She couldn't help wondering if this was part of some conspiracy, if this excess of access was a form of sleight of hand. *Look over here, look how much you can find. Pay no attention to the man behind the curtain.* H. L. Mencken had despised those who never left the newsroom, calling them the castrati of the craft.

Then again, Mencken had boasted about making things up, so he was a problematic role model.

Still, her confinement—Lord, how old-fashioned—unnerved her. She trusted Mrs. Blossom, but no one's eyes saw exactly what she saw. And while her instincts were far from unerring, they were *her* instincts. If she had visited Don Epstein, she would have a better sense of the man. She was quick to recognize a liar even when she couldn't pinpoint the lie. But she was stuck here, with an Italian greyhound who moaned incessantly and a taskmaster in amniotic fluid. Lately, she and Crow had taken to calling the baby "Fifi La Pew," one of those stupid couples jokes that come out of nowhere, only to stick. In fact, Crow was becoming enamored with "Fifi" as a possible name. Tess imagined trying to explain this to her parents. *Here's your granddaughter, Fifi Monaghan.* It was a toss-up which name would make her conventional mother crazier.

The baby would be a Monaghan. Crow, who was almost *too* evolved, had decided that the child, as a girl, should have Tess's surname. She could not deny that she was happy about this. Of course, her name was her father's name. They could use her mother's "maiden" name—Fifi Weinstein had quite the ring to it—but that was a man's name, too, in the end. To find a true maiden name, one would have to go back to Lilith, Tess supposed. Poor Lilith, the original first wife, doomed to be forgotten.

She glanced again at the copy of the marriage license that Mrs. Blossom had left behind. Carole Epstein had been Carole Massinger. She plugged the latter into Google, finally scoring a hit on a Web site maintained by a freelance photographer. There was Carole Massinger, in a photograph taken at a wedding. The photo seemed a little fake, stagy, as photos in such settings often do, but it was definitely the woman Tess had seen through her binoculars. The hair was different, but she wore a dress of celery green, and brandished—did this woman coordinate *everything*?—a pale green cocktail. Her smile was broad, genuine. She was toasting the beaming groom and his bride, whom the photographer had helpfully identified as Don and Annette Epstein.

Chapter 4

"Of course he married someone else he already knew, Tess," Dorie Starnes said. "That's what men *do*. Most men can't function alone."

"Still, it's eerie, especially now that his second wife has disappeared—"

"Ah, but you're wrong on that."

"How can you be so sure?"

"I'll explain in all in due time. You don't rush a master. You've made nice progress, with your laptop and your phone, but it's nothing compared to what I can do with a couple of hours of computer time."

When had Dorie Starnes, once an ignored and scorned IT grunt at the local newspaper, learned to speak with such emphatic authority—and on all subjects, yet, not just computers? But Tess knew, for she had been a part of Dorie's transformation. When they met five years ago, Dorie had no sense of her own power. Tess had shown her how much she knew, how much potential she had, giving her the confidence to open her own research firm, now a thriving concern. Despite that, Tess didn't even get a discount on Dorie's not inconsiderable hourly rate. All she got were "bumping rights"—priority over Dorie's other customers, without having to pay rush rates. Normally, that was all Tess needed, given that she could pass the cost on to her clients. But who was her client in this matter, who would reimburse her? The insane Italian greyhound was clearly indigent; Carole Massinger Esptein was missing—only not according to her husband. She would have to pay for Dorie's services out of her own pocket. *Sorry, Fifi. That's a few dollars less for the college fund.*

"Annette Epstein had been married to Don Epstein for almost five years when she died," Dorie began, reading from her laptop. She would have preferred a PowerPoint presentation, no doubt, but Tess's sun porch wasn't set up for that.

"What was the cause?"

"Pneumonia was listed as the official cause, although that was actually a complication that resulted after her hospitalization. She died in an Anne Arundel hospital about eighteen months ago. Her husband sued, charging wrongful death. Hospital settled out of court."

"For how much?"

Dorie shook her head. A short, top-heavy woman, she always reminded Tess of a robin, with her rounded front and tousled hair. In fact, just looking at her made Tess want to burst into the opening of "My Funny Valentine," the prologue that so few people knew, in which the gentleman's blank countenance was compared to a bird's. But there was nothing vacant about Dorie's brow. Like Mrs. Blossom, Dorie was another person the world tended to underestimate. Tess was surrounded by such people, she realized. She was one, in fact, a broad-shouldered jockette. Strangers would have trusted her with a lacrosse stick, but not much else.

"I'm not *that* good," Dorrie said. "Out-of-court settlements are sealed, and this one included a gag order. If Esptein shared the details, the hospital could reclaim its payment. But let's play connect the dots. Epstein filed the lawsuit just before the deadline ran out. Settlement was reached in April of this year and he closed on the house on Blythewood in July. For cash—$1.2 million."

"Couldn't part of the payment come from equity in his previous home? That house was appraised at four million."

"He owned the previous house only four years, and the sale price was only slightly above the price he paid. Figure in closing costs, and it was a zero-sum game for him. And according to documents he filed in the lawsuit, in which he was trying to demonstrate actual costs related to his wife's death, he said he tapped into equity to cover her hospital bills."

"No insurance?"

Dorie smiled. "No *health* insurance. He neglected to add her to the plan he carries through his job, and the insurance company was fighting him every step of the way over that bureaucratic oversight. Yet he didn't overlook the life insurance. The hospital's lawyers included that in their findings. His lawyer countered by putting in a claim for the wife's personal property, including a $20,000 engagement ring they say was stolen in the hospital. He eventually got $500,000, so part of that could have gone to pay for the house on Blythewood."

Tess clicked back to the photo of the happy couple on their wedding day, studied the ring, an Art Deco monstrosity bordered by a darker stone.

"It's big," she said. "Does that make it worth twenty thousand?"

"If the hospital didn't challenge him, he can claim any amount he wanted."

Tess yearned to study these files herself, to pore over every detail. It would be dull, tedious work, but she might see something that Dorie had missed. Dorie was essentially a human search engine. She worked from known parameters, finding only what she was asked to find.

"You said the pneumonia was a complication subsequent to her admission. Why was she in the hospital?"

"She had been in and out of the hospital for idiopathic fever and nausea for much of the previous year. The last time around, she developed a staph infection and pneumonia."

"Idiot fever?"

"*Idiopathic.* No known cause. She was a bit of a medical mystery, as the hospital freely admits. Don Epstein's lawyer argued that it was the hospital's fault, because she must have contacted staph while hospitalized, and that made her more vulnerable to pneumonia. There's a lot of stuff in the filings about her use of antibiotics. He swore she didn't, the hospital contends she did and concealed it. In the end, they settled."

The fact of a settlement proved nothing. The hospital might have settled because it was cheaper, in the long run. Don Epstein might have settled because he knew he didn't have a good case. Whatever grief he felt over his wife, he seemed to have assuaged it quickly, with a new house and a new wife.

But then—widowers were considered desirable, and Carole Massinger had been a friend, close enough to attend his wedding. Tess had known other widowers who found new loves within a year of their wives' deaths. Dorie was right: Most men sucked at being alone.

Then again, Tess didn't know a single widower whose new wife had gone into the woods one day and never been seen again. And, thanks to Mrs. Blossom, she knew that Carole Epstein had yet to put in an appearance at the house on Blythewood Lane. She herself had called the home number several times, using a cell phone whose number was shielded from caller ID. She either got the machine, with a young woman's voice—light and silvery as Gatsby's Daisy—promising to get back to her, or the real-life Don Epstein who said Carole was out of town and, no, he didn't know when she would be back, and just who was calling, anyway? So far, Tess had called as a member of Carole Epstein's book club, curious to find out if she had read *The Kite Runner* yet. (No, she didn't know if Carole Epstein was even in a book club, but she wagered that Don Epstein didn't, either.) She had called as a saleswoman, eager to tell Carole about new arrivals at a local boutique; a woman who bought matching raincoats for herself and her Italian greyhound clearly cared about the latest shipment of Marc Jacobs. And she had called as the breeder, checking up on little—well, what did you name the dog, Mr. Epstein?

"She calls it Dempsey," he had said.

"After the boxer?" she'd asked him.

"After the actor, the one on that doctor show, that all the women think is so cute."

"And is Dempsey settling in—"

"It's my wife's dog. You'll have to talk to her."

"Certainly. When will she be in?"

"She's away on business. I expect her next week."

He was unwavering on this fact: Carole was away on business. He expected her next week. The thing was, he had been saying this for two weeks now.

Now, Tess asked Dorie: "Did you find out anything else about the first Mrs. Epstein?"

Her smile was triumphant. "Oh, indeed. You would have, too, if the *Beacon-Light* online archives went back just a little further. You see, Annette wasn't the first Mrs. Epstein, she was the second. You're actually looking for the third Mrs. Epstein. And the first Mrs. Epstein was a straight-up homicide victim."

Now that was quite a rabbit to pull from one's hat. No wonder Dorie had been preening so.

The photocopied newspaper clippings that Dorie produced reminded Tess just how many times the

Beacon-Light had redesigned itself over the past fifteen years, paying more attention to its fonts and columns than it ever did to its local reporting. These clips were evidence of its more sober, serious past, when the front page held up to eight stories. In 1994, the date on the photocopied clip, most of the articles were national and international, as befit a newspaper that took itself oh-so-seriously.

But there was always room on the front page for the deadly carjacking of a couple from Greenspring Valley—code for "rich, white"—when they took an ill-advised shortcut coming home from the theater and found themselves on Greenmount Avenue—again, locals would recognize this as shorthand for "poor, black"—and someone attempted to steal their Mercedes just outside the gates of the cemetery that held John Wilkes Booth. The inclusion of that stray detail baffled Tess, but the reporter seemed to think it was relevant because the couple had attended a performance of *Assassins* at the Morris Mechanic Theater. Tess was surprised the writer hadn't tried to make some rhetorical hay out of the Greenmount/Greenspring dichotomy.

Mrs. Epstein had been shot in the head, while Mr. Epstein had been shot in the leg. The assailant was described as a "young man in baggy pants."

"Sound familiar now?" Dorie asked.

"I would have been in college," Tess said. "And I hate to admit it, but when I was in college on the Eastern Shore, I wouldn't have paid attention to a murder back in Baltimore. In fact, I would have considered these people *old.*" Don and Mary Epstein were thirty-nine at the time.

"No, not this particular case. The scenario. Because it sure sounded familiar to Baltimore cops back then. It was six years after Charles Stuart, up in Boston. Wife killed, guy injured, but so severely that no one could believe he did it to himself. Epstein almost bled to death because the bullet hit the femoral artery. But Epstein runs a chain of check-cashing stores, stores he inherited from his first wife's dad, as it happens. He probably never studied anatomy."

"So he was a suspect?"

"Never officially, but you'll see in the clips how cagey the police are, how careful they are not to inflame things. For one—the race of the suspect isn't specified. No one was ever charged and the car was found about a mile away, abandoned, and while they took a lot of fingerprints, the only hits they got were on Epstein and his wife."

One man, three wives. Two dead, one missing. One killed in a homicide, one dead after a mysterious illness lands her in a hospital, which claims that it could have taken better care of her if they had been informed of her excessive use of antibiotics. But why would the second Mrs. Epstein have withheld this information? The media had been almost hysterical over staph infections at the time. Who would fail to disclose her use of antibiotics, knowing she was at risk for MSRA?

Possibly a woman who didn't know she had been taking antibiotics.

"Who was the primary on the Epstein investigation, the carjacking?"

"Harold Lenhardt. Still a cop, but out in the county now. He left a year or two after this happened."

A nursery rhyme played in Tess's head: *When I was going to St. Ives, I met a man with seven wives.* Only in her version, it became: *When I was going to St. Ives, I met a man who lost three wives.*

Three makes a trend, as she'd learned in her newspaper days, and if Carole Epstein was dead, it was a hard trend to ignore. Being married to Don Epstein carried a shockingly high mortality rate.

But of the three, the one indisputable homicide was the first Mrs. Epstein. She would start there.

Sergeant Harold Lenhardt sounded friendly when she finally tracked him down by phone. He remained friendly for about thirty seconds, when Tess explained why she had called.

"I don't talk about that."

"But—"

"I'm not allowed to talk about it."

"Lawsuit?" There was no gag order on the homicide, as far as Tess knew, just on the settlement involving the second wife's death.

"I don't *allow* myself to talk about it," he amended.

"But—"

"Look, I just don't."

"But—"

"You're not the first reporter to call. You won't be the last."

"I'm not a reporter. I'm a private investigator. Don Epstein's first wife was murdered. His second wife died in a hospital. Now his third wife is missing, and he's pretending she's not."

"A third wife? He's got a third wife now?"

"Did. As I said, he seems remarkably unperturbed by the fact that she left on a business trip and has yet to come home."

"Damn," he said. Then: "Excuse me."

"I've heard worse. I've *said* much worse."

"Me, too. But I try to watch myself in front of ladies."

Tess didn't think she had ever been called a lady before. She was torn between being charmed and wanting to demonstrate her own prodigious talent for cursing.

"Couldn't we just have a conversation?"

"Epstein tried to sue me for slander. It didn't go anywhere—you can't sue a detective for doing his job—but he's had me on notice for years. He sued the paper for libel at the time, too. Got thrown out on summary judgment, but he's a litigious"—a pause, as he caught himself on the verge of a much harsher noun—"SOB."

"No one has to know we spoke," Tess said.

"You mentioned three wives. Do you know about Danielle? "

"Danielle?"

A heavy sigh, the beginning of another burst or profanity quickly swallowed. "She was his girlfriend, between wives one and two. And yeah, she's dead, too, which is on my conscience, because I couldn't nail the"—another pause—"SOB. Now you tell me there's two more on the ledger because I couldn't close. Damn. Sorry. Okay, we'll talk."

Chapter 5

Tess had never had particularly excitable hormones. Cranky as a child—she had earned her sometimes nickname of Testy—she mellowed with age. Even the demons of PMS didn't notably alter her moods. But pregnancy was different. And, perhaps because she was forced to sit still, the energy that was supposed to be forming her so-far-missing maternal instincts was beginning to manifest itself in odd and unexpected ways. Mood swings? Try mood teeter-totters, mood elevators, mood escalators, mood rockets. Add a daily dose of *Oprah* and *Judge Judy* to the mix and she was truly unpredictable.

Take, for example, the crush she developed on Sergeant Harold Lenhardt the moment he walked through her door. He was stocky, at least twenty years older than she—which made him almost twenty-five years older than Crow—and had nothing in common with any man to whom she had been drawn before. Yet she liked him instantaneously, and even tried flirting with him, after a fashion.

It was, she decided, all about eye contact. Harold Lenhardt locked eyes with a woman as if there were no other person in the world to whom he would rather speak. She found herself babbling to him—oversharing, as the current phrase had it—telling him in great detail how she had come to sit here, watching the woman she now knew to be Carole Esptein.

"It doesn't make sense that she would abandon a dog on whom she clearly doted." Dempsey's toenails clattered against the bars. "Even a dog as insane as this one has turned out to be."

"He's not insane," Lenhardt said. "No bad dogs, right? Just bad people." And before she could object, he opened the crate and coaxed Dempsey out. The dog immediately wet the floor, and Lenhardt went to the kitchen and found cleaning supplies. Even so, his manner with the dog was firm, but gentle, and Dempsey responded, albeit in an odd way: He walked over to the porcelain chamber pot, the gift from Tess's aunt, and continued urinating there.

"He's a little too spirited for you in your current, uh, condition," Lenhardt said. "But he's trainable."

"He may have been the last person—well, not person, but mammal—to see Carole Epstein alive, I fear."

"Yeah, about that." He drew a chair close to Tess's chaise longue, the better to make his signature eye contact. "I checked. She hasn't been reported missing. You can't *make* a man say his wife is missing, you know. He says she's on a business trip, who's going to contradict him? You need to find a family member, or a friend to start agitating."

"My suspicions aren't enough?"

"They could be, but what you've told me is kinda flimsy. Besides, this is not a man to anger. He's insanely litigious, a real SOB. Do not get in his crosshairs. The guy tried to sue me for slander. When that failed, he tried to get my neighbors to sue me over property lines. He'll come at people any way he can, once he's angry. He likes to win, at any cost."

"Do you think he murdered his first wife?"

Lenhardt looked around, as if he couldn't be certain that they were alone. "First, let me tell you how paranoid I am about this guy. I didn't come here until I did a lot of checking on you. A lot. I thought he might be playing me, trying to set me up. And, you know, he lives on just the other side of that hill from you. But you checked out, so I'm here. And I think you're right to be worried about his third wife. But this is not a guy you tangle with lightly."

"Did you suspect him right away?"

Dempsey came over to Lenhardt and presented his snout, nosing at the sergeant's hand until he got the point and began scratching him behind the ears. Tess's hormones hissed with jealousy.

"Yeah. Here's the weird thing. He kept insisting that the kid who 'jacked him was white. Which in that neighborhood is a little farfetched, statistically. Oh, it could have been some suburban kid, come down to cop, but why would that kid need to steal a car, and why would he dump it nearby? I felt like, after the stuff that happened with Charles Stuart and Susan Smith—she was just a few months before—Epstein was trying to be a PC faker. But he stuck to the story—scrawny white kid, in a hooded sweatshirt, ran in front of his car, flagged him down. He stopped because he thought the kid was in trouble. He got out, was shot in the leg. Missus gets out of the car, she gets shot in the head, twice. Kid drives the car maybe four blocks, dumps it."

"So if it's not an accident—he has an accomplice."

"Right. At first, I thought it was the woman he started dating a few months later. But she died two years later. Accident at home. Tripped over her own cat, fell down the stairs."

"That was Danielle, the one you mentioned on the phone?"

He nodded. "Danielle. She was so pretty . . ." Again, that strange flush of jealousy. Did Lenhardt think Tess was pretty? Could anyone think she was pretty in this state?

"The thing is—I was working her really hard, the month before the accident. I thought she knew something. She was his bookkeeper. And one thing I noticed, whenever I talked to her, is that she would be very adamant about when they started dating. 'You know, we didn't start dating until the winter, in January.' Every time, that came up. So I said to her one day: 'Yeah, you didn't start dating until three months after his wife was killed, but before she was killed, were you screwing around?' That rattled her, I think."

"Did she ever admit they were having an affair?"

"No, she never did. But she knew something. And when she died—well, I thought it was my fault, that I should have been more insistent, gotten her to see the kind of guy she was dating. She had had a tough life. Parents dead in a car accident when she was barely in her twenties, left to raise her kid sister, almost ten years younger than she was. Other than her involvement with Epstein, she seemed like a really good person."

He fingered the quilt. "Geese in Flight," he said. "Nice." Then, at Tess's surprised look: "My wife, she's into stuff like this, although she's younger than me, by a bit. Used to be a nurse. That's who cops meet—nurses, state's attorneys, other cops. Waitresses. Everyone says I'm punching way above my weight class with her. She's gorgeous. But, hey, I needed to sweeten the genetic pot for my kids, you know?"

Tess's hormones sighed, thwarted.

"Did you know your wife was the one, the moment you met her?" she asked. "Or did it creep up on you?" Her relationship with Crow fell in the latter camp, and she couldn't help thinking there was something special about the thunderbolt school of love.

"I knew she was good-looking, the moment I saw her. That's hard to miss. But, as I said, she's younger. And I had been married before, screwed that up. I didn't believe in second chances. I kept looking for the *catch*. She was pretty, she was good company. Why was she available? Why did she want to go with me? Eventually, I decided to stop questioning my good luck and just grab it. We've been together eighteen years now."

Tess had lost the thread of what Lenhardt was saying. She couldn't get over the fact that Don Epstein's girlfriend had sat in a room with this man and not told him everything. She knew she would have told him whatever he wanted to know. She wanted, in fact, to confess all her transgressions to him—the time she sneaked out in her father's car and smashed the tail light, the marijuana she smoked as recently as four months ago—before she knew she was pregnant—the various laws she had bent and even broken in her own line of work.

Then she got it. This wasn't all hormonal. Lenhardt was a good murder police, a good one, in or out of the box. On some level, he was always in the box, always working it, inspiring people to confide in him. It was a habit he couldn't break. The 7-Eleven cashier probably tried to tell him her life story when he bought a cup of coffee.

"Do you have children?"

"A boy and a girl," he said. "And a girl from my first marriage."

"Do your kids tell you everything?"

"The boy does. The girl—the girl could glide through Guantanamo and never crack. My older girl—she hasn't talked to me for almost twenty years."

"I'm having a girl."

"My condolences." He smiled. "Seriously, you'll love it. Parenthood, I mean. I'm not calling your child an 'it.' "

"Promise I'll love it?"

"I do, in fact. I promise that you'll love it, you'll hate it, that it will be your greatest joy. And show you a new level of fear, too. I just hope it won't be your greatest sorrow as well. Me, I've known both."

He got up to leave. "Find a family member or a friend, someone who will take this to the police. You know her maiden name, by any chance?"

"Yes, it's . . ." She flipped through the pages she had been collecting. ". . . Massinger."

A queer look crossed Lenhardt's face. "Are you sure?"

"It's on her marriage certificate."

"Because that was Danielle's last name, too."

Danielle Messinger had died—accidentally, according to the autopsy—after tripping over her cat. Her sister, Carole, twenty at the time, was in her junior year at Salisbury State. In fact, it was Carole's panicky call that had prompted a neighbor to check on Danielle, who had not answered her phone on Easter Sunday. Danielle had been dead for several days, presumably falling on Good Friday, with no chance of resurrection.

Why hadn't her boss—and boyfriend—been similarly worried? She had the four-day weekend off, Don

Epstein told police. Danielle said she had plans. No, he didn't know what they were. She had been kind of secretive lately, moody and distracted. Truth was, they had a fight Wednesday night and she had been giving him the silent treatment. He didn't attend the funeral, but then—there was no funeral to attend. Danielle Messinger's sister had returned to Severna Park, taken charge of her sister's remains and had her cremated.

That was as much as Lenhardt could tell Tess, after she showed him the photo of Carole with Don Epstein and his second wife, toasting them at their wedding.

"Did she know him then?" Tess asked. "I mean back then, when her sister died."

"Knew *of* him, as I recall, but mainly in the context of her sister's boss. She was in college when they started dating. She did say they were engaged, which was news to me. And to Epstein, who denied it, and the fact was, there was no ring on her finger, no proof. That said, I always thought Epstein was keen to marry Danielle, if only for spousal immunity. She knew *something*. She had agreed to meet with me the following week."

Dusk had fallen by now, the dogs and their walkers had come and gone. Tess had encouraged Lenhardt to pour himself a drink, and tried not to be too envious of the Jameson to which he helped himself. She didn't even *like* Jameson, but the fact that she couldn't have it made it all too desirable.

"Okay, but—" The door opened. Tess had to leave it unlocked when she expected visitors, not to mention the delivery of her meals. It was her supper, brought tonight by Crow's acolyte, Lloyd Jupiter. Once a street kid, all jangly nerves and bravado, he had found a vocation and sense of direction at Crow's alma mater, the Maryland Institute College of Art, where he was studying film on scholarship. He also was dating a stunningly beautiful Chinese girl, one adopted at age two and raised by two mommies. All of this—an Asian girl, her gay parents, school—represented so much growth for Lloyd that Tess was almost wistful for the brash, skeptical teenager he had been not that long ago. It was a relief of sorts to see the face he made as he entered with the carryout from Dukem, the Ethiopian restaurant. Lloyd remained closed off to all culinary experiences outside of cheeseburgers, chicken boxes, and pizza.

"You could not pay me to eat this—" He stopped short when he saw Lenhardt. "Why is there a police here? Did you find that crazy dog's owner?"

Lloyd, also picking up the slack in the dog-walking department, had been bitten by Dempsey and now wanted nothing to do with him. He took Esskay and Miata out happily, but refused to walk Dempsey.

"Sergeant Harold Lenhardt. He is a cop, but he's also a miracle worker with dogs. Look how calm Dempsey is."

Dempsey, nestled against the mountain that was Tess's belly, bared his teeth at Lloyd and growled.

"Dog's a flat-out racist," Lloyd said.

"He hates everyone," Tess points out.

"Hates everyone. Bit *me*."

Lloyd began to arrange the food on Tess's bed tray, and she was careful to mask her amazement. Gushing over Lloyd's transformation tended to make him revert to his most thuggish, surly behavior. Left alone, without comment, he increasingly did the right thing in the right way. She had no idea why a curriculum of watching films and attempting to make them would produce such a change in a person. May, who had been assigned to tutor Lloyd when he struggled with the required English class, probably deserved some credit too. Tess watched him matter-of-factly taking out the blood pressure cuff and fastening it to her arm.

"Maybe you should consider medical school."

He snorted as if this were a joke on Tess's part, as if he didn't realize that he had come so far that medical school would not be that much of a reach. He wrote down her pressure in the pad that Crow kept by the bed, then went to the kitchen to get her a glass of water.

"Corner kid," Lenhardt said, in the same diagnostic tone in which Lloyd had pronounced him police.

"Was," Tess said. "Not anymore."

"It's hard," Lenhardt said, "for people to change."

"Yet they do, sometimes. Maybe Don Epstein changed, and Carole really is on a business trip. Maybe he's just a really unlucky guy."

"Maybe," Lenhardt said.

"Maybe he's just snakebit."

"Maybe," Lenhardt said, "and maybe, if I eat enough barbecued spare ribs at the Corner Stable, a pig will fly out of my butt."

Chapter 6

How can I miss you if you won't go away, Dan Hicks and his Hot Licks once asked. Similarly, Tess was finding out that it's hard to be a missing person if no one will admit to missing you. Yet, try as she might, she couldn't find anyone—a friend, a relative, a co-worker—who could make a credible complaint about the disappearance of Carole Epstein. There appeared to be no one in her life except Don Epstein. Oh, Tess had enough drag to get the cops to make a duty call, to question Epstein without revealing the source of the inquiry. But Epstein produced e-mails from his wife and even text messages. Easily faked, as far as Tess was concerned—if he had done away with Carole Epstein, he would have her phone and could send the text messages himself. And many spouses had access to each other's e-mail.

But unless someone close to Carole insisted she had been the victim of foul play, there was little else that police could do. She was on a business trip. Her husband said she was a handbag designer, just getting started, and she was visiting small stores that she hoped would carry her designs. Dempsey appeared to be the only one to notice her absence—how else to explain his strange behavior? Otherwise, no one cared.

"It's all very existential," Whitney agreed. "If a wife falls down in the forest, does she make a sound? I wonder how many days I could be gone without anyone noticing."

"You live with your parents."

"On their property, not in their house," Whitney said. "I could fall in the bathtub and be there for days. Days! Squirrels would come down the fireplace and start nibbling at my body. Did you tell the police about Mr. Epstein's incredibly bad luck with the fair sex?"

"Yes, and they didn't write me off as a complete kook. That's why they were willing to talk to him at all. But that's as far as they'll go right now. There's no public pressure, no media attention whatsoever."

"Why would someone marry her sister's older boyfriend? That's kind of icky."

Tess had a theory. But then, at this point there was little about the Epsteins that she had not thought through. The girl in the green raincoat filled her imagination. In a sense, she now spent more time in the company of Carole Epstein than with anyone else. Unless one counted Dempsey.

"It does happen—a loved one is lost, and a new relationship forms between the two people who grieved over that person. After all, it's been almost fifteen years ago Danielle Messinger died, and Carole was only twenty at the time. He even had another wife in between, and Carole apparently socialized with them as a couple. As a friend, she might have offered him moral support after Annette's death, and that turned to love."

"Romantic," Whitney said. "Perfectly innocuous. Do you happen to believe it?"

"I might—if it weren't for this dog."

Whitney stretched out on the floor, and Dempsey, who had taken to sleeping at Tess's feet, jumped down and inspected her, then began to growl. Tess remembered Lenhardt's crash course and asserted herself as the alpha dog. "No, Dempsey." The dog shot her an irritated look, but returned to his spot on the bed. He was getting better, but the other dogs still loathed him and had to spend their days locked in the bedroom.

"There's one thing that doesn't fit," Whitney said. "This friendless, isolated woman in your scenario? You said she was always on her cell phone when she walked her dog. Who, pray tell, was she talking to?"

Tess conjured up the image of what she had seen—Carole Epstein in her green raincoat, hand cupped to her ear, always in conversation. Tess had judged her for that, just a little. That initial judgment seemed unfair now, as initial judgments often tend to be.

"Maybe her husband had her on a figurative leash, and required that she check in," she said.

"She had a lover," Whitney said. "A lover or a confidante. If Don Epstein is the monster you think he is, any kind of confidante would have unnerved him. The mere fact of a secret relationship, even a nonsexual one, would have bothered him."

"Especially if she had information that could connect him to a homicide. I think she knew something, Whitney, and that's why she had to disappear."

Whitney paged through Tess's file. Tess always kept her work in an orderly fashion, but this file, entered into the black-and-white Roaring Springs composition books that Tess had always favored, was a masterpiece of color-coding and charting. She had a lot of time on her hands, after all.

"Nice car," Whitney said, stopping on the page with all the MVA data on the Epsteins. "And you know what? I think LoJack was being offered as a sweetener on that model for a while. I got a flyer from the dealer. As if I would spend that kind of money on a car."

"So?"

"God, you're slow. Is the baby keeping oxygen from getting to your brain? If Carole's driving to boutiques up and down the eastern seaboard, as her husband insists, then LoJack will confirm his story. But if she's disappeared, then she's not driving her car, and it's parked somewhere. Get Martin Tull, your cop friend, to engage the device."

It wasn't quite as easy as Whitney made it sound, but Detective Tull eventually found the dealership and convinced it to track the car. Carole Epstein's green BMW was discovered in the parking garage at Baltimore Penn Station. The electronic ticket in the well between the front seats established that it had been there since the evening of the day that Tess saw her last. Her keys had been left in the ignition of the unlocked car, dangling from a Gucci key chain that should have been temptation enough unto itself. Impossible to say why the keys hadn't been taken, but it was easy to establish why the car hadn't been—the alternator was on the fritz.

Police returned to the home of Don Epstein that night, local television crews not far behind. In an impromptu press conference on his lawn, a red-eyed Epstein announced: "She left me. I just learned today that she's stolen thousands of dollars from me. The e-mails, the texts—I have to assume they were all cover, so she could continue cleaning out our joint accounts. She left me and covered her tracks, just to get a head start on bleeding me dry."

Tess, watching from her chaise longue, threw her hands up in frustration. Crow got out the blood-pressure cuff.

"He's telling the truth about the accounts," Martin Tull said. "She did it electronically, transferring money to an Internet-based bank, then moving that money to an account we can't find, probably offshore."

"It was a joint account," Tess said. "He could have done it."

"If he did, he didn't use his home computer. The ISP doesn't match."

"Doesn't match his *home* computer, but how do you know he doesn't have a secret laptop? He runs a check-cashing business, Martin. He probably knows a few tricks about how to move money around."

Tull was a murder police, one of the best. But he also was a friend, and Tess was beginning to realize he was here in that role, indulging the hysterical pregnant woman.

"She could have taken light rail to BWI," he said. "She's probably got a whole second identity, which is why her credit cards and ATM have been dormant."

"And he could have a conspirator," she insisted. "Based on history, he already has his next wife lined up. Cherchez la femme, Martin. He gets rid of them when he tires of them, probably to avoid alimony. If Carole Epstein managed to siphon all that money out of their joint accounts, then she's the first one to walk away with a nickel. The rest all walked away dead, if you will. And what about the car at Penn Station, the keys? *He* could have left it there, gone home on the number sixty-one bus."

"Look, we're not saying he's in the clear," Tull said. "Not at all. And we would like Mrs. Epstein to show up, explain a few things. Then again, she has a very plausible reason not to come forward, right? If the guy's right, she's on an island somewhere."

It would be a good revenge plot of sorts, Tess thought, if Carole Epstein believed that Don had killed her sister yet couldn't prove it. But would she settle for money? Would that begin to approximate justice? No, Tess believed this woman had bigger fish to fry.

"She left her dog behind," Tess said. "Knowing Don Epstein as she does, she never would have left Dempsey in his care."

"She let go of her dog's leash, assuming it would find a good home when she made a run for it," Tull said. "And it has."

Dempsey looked up, as if aware that he was the topic of conversation, then went back to gnawing on his own haunch. The dog had an amazing repertoire of neurotic tics. He chewed his own legs, worried his lower lip, scratched himself raw in places.

"The vet says he has emotional issues," Tess said. "Sort of like those adolescent girls that cut themselves."

"Yeah," Tull said, "who wouldn't take that dog along on her new life?"

He had a point.

"Look," he added. "I agree this all stinks. And we've put out the word that we'd like to hear from her—and not by e-mail or text message. But what else can we do? There's no evidence of foul play on his part."

"Does he have an alibi for the day she disappeared?"

"He says he was stuck in traffic on the Beltway. But there was a lot of publicity about an overturned tractor-trailer on the outer loop that afternoon, so he could be making it up. Thing is, hard as it is for him to prove he was there, we can't disprove it."

"He never uses the same method twice," Tess said. "A carjacking, a fall, a mysterious infection that could have been avoided if the hospital knew the patient was taking antibiotics. He's got a good imagination."

"Yeah, well," Tull said. "He's not the only one."

Don Epstein was on television but just a local show. Even the cable networks that seemed devoted to covering missing white women 24/7 didn't care about Epstein. It was the runaway bride story, played out before it even started: missing/faker/skank. At least this one reporter, one of the few enterprising investigative reporters on local television, was skeptical of him. *So much bad luck, for one man. Did he feel cursed? Had he considered forswearing the company of women, given how badly it seemed to end for him, every time? Was he sure that his wife hadn't been the victim of foul play, that the computer transfers of money had been done by someone else with access to her laptop?*

Yet Don Epstein preened, happy in the spotlight, indifferent to the subtext. Yes, he had been unlucky in love, he told the reporter. He did wonder if he was cursed, if he should take himself out of the dating pool. Even as he was speaking, a woman e-mailed the studio and the reporter read her comment on air: "I'd take a chance on you, Don. Call me!"

Tess could not fathom this. Why would anyone want Don Epstein under any circumstances? What did he have to offer any woman? Money, yes—although he had less than he once had, if one believed that Carole Epstein had absconded with almost half his savings. Still, it was a substantial fortune. He wasn't bad-looking, if one's taste ran to the overly virile and hirsute. Still, there was the fact of three wives, one girlfriend, all dead. Well, three dead and one missing. Were women really this desperate?

She had recently read an article that applied gaming theory to the eternal topic of why there were so many great single women. Again, as all such articles did, it concluded that women should just settle. Yet she couldn't recall anything that advised men to settle. They were the ones encouraged to hold out for everything, and to trade up to a new, flashier model.

"I know our age difference doesn't matter to you now," she said to Crow that evening, "but don't you think you'll find it a drag to be married to a, say, fifty-year-old when you're forty-four?"

"I am going to take the television away," Crow said. "Between *Oprah* and *Judge Judy*, you are just loaded for bear by the time I come home."

"I wonder if they're still checking Carole Epstein's credit cards."

"I'm sure they are." It was becoming Crow's weary refrain.

"And her debit card, too. What other marks do we leave in this world? How else can we be traced?"

"Try to settle down, Tess."

But "settle down" reminded her of *settling*, period, and she was furious again. Dissatisfied by conversation with Crow, she decided to talk to her daughter, who seemed to be kicking her feet rhythmically, as antsy about confinement as Dempsey.

Don't ever settle, Fifi. Don't get married just because it's still marketed as the ultimate achievement for women.

On the other hand, learn to value men for something other than their paychecks. Your father was a bookstore clerk and an underemployed musician when we started dating. Now he's a partner in a restaurant/bar with good music every weekend. He still doesn't make much money, though. I support us. Or did, before you put the kibosh on everything. Do you realize how much your college fund will miss these extra weeks of work I've had to sacrifice? Do you know about compound interest yet? Look, in today's economy, you need to start putting stuff away in the womb.

Yet the economy was good for private detectives. More small businesses suspected theft among their employees. Insurance fraud was rampant. Even with Mrs. Blossom as a partner, she was doing fine.

Don Epstein—Don Epstein, on the other hand, owned check-cashing stores. Check-cashing stores that had belonged to his first wife's father, but became his exclusively when she died. She wondered if these stores thrived in the current economy, or if they had a lot of defaults. She wondered if Carole Epstein had life insurance. She wondered how long someone had to go missing before you could collect on life insurance. She wondered—

But perhaps she had worn herself out, or her future daughter had decided enough was enough and Mom needed to go down for a nap. She fell asleep at the disgracefully early hour of 9:00 P.M. *Snapshot of your future*, as Whitney might have said. Except for the ten hours of sleep that followed.

Chapter 7

Tess Monaghan did not always appreciate her parents as much as she should. Who ever has? In her childhood, her mother was . . . well, a mother, an obstacle to be surmounted. Judith Monaghan also had an unfortunate predilection for overmatching. Shoes matched purse matched dress matched earrings matched bracelets. A secretary at the National Security Agency, she insisted she could never speak of her job at home, hinting that she was privy to too many secrets.

But as Tess moved into her thirties, she began to discern that her mother's wardrobe was the result of a fiercely misdirected energy. Born a mere decade later, Judith Weinstein Monaghan might have been given a chance to apply her impeccable sense of organization to . . . well, whatever NSA did. (Despite reading

The Puzzle Palace, Tess was still fuzzy on the details.) Meanwhile, growing up with a maybe-spy for a mother had the happy bonus of sharpening Tess's wits, teaching her to be a much more sophisticated sneak.

As for her father, Patrick Monaghan, the world's most taciturn Irishman, Tess had once yearned for him to be everything he was not—voluble, dashing, a literary bon vivant who held forth on the work of James Joyce. If she wasn't such a snob then, she might have noticed she'd been graced with Wonder Dad, who could fix or build anything. Instead, she had taken it all as her due—the sturdy, safe tire swing that drew the neighborhood children to her house, the gleaming bicycles on Christmas morning, which her father put together swiftly and quietly, without any profanity-laden outbursts to waken a sleeping girl from dreams of Santa. He had, in fact, contributed much of the work to this sun porch where she now spent her days. Now Tess was thrilled to have a father who could wield a hammer. She didn't need to talk about Joyce. The fact was, she really didn't have a lot to say about Joyce, and there were always things that required fixing.

Today, her father was installing a dog door on the lower level, while one of his old cronies finished securing the perimeter with invisible fencing. These additions were for the unwalkable Dempsey, who had taken to relieving himself almost exclusively in the porcelain chamber pot, which meant that Tess was often trapped for hours in a room that smelled of dog urine. The hope was that Dempsey could be trained quickly to understand how far he could roam in the yard without receiving a mild shock, via the radio transmitter.

He did catch on quickly. But to everyone's dismay, Dempsey seemed to *enjoy* the sensation. He threw himself at the boundary again and again, yelping in outrage and pain, yet never trying to leave.

"Dog's a little strange," said Tess's father, watching the scene through her window. He was not only taciturn, but given to understatement.

"He's testing himself," Tess said. "Notice that he doesn't try to leave. I thought he'd made a run for it, head back to Blythewood. He's letting us know that he's here on his own recognizance."

Dempsey, satisfied that he had shown the fence line who was boss, trotted through his new door and clacked upstairs to the sun porch—where he promptly squatted over the chamber pot and relieved himself.

"I brought you a gift, by the way," her father said.

"Something for the baby?" Tess asked warily. Her father was having a hard time with her decision not to prepare in advance. He wanted to buy a crib and a stroller, build a toy chest and a changing table, paint the spare bedroom. And, in time, she wanted him to do all those things. But not yet.

"No, this is for you." He went to the living room and returned with a large flat package, wrapped in newspaper and string.

"The sign from the Stonewall Democratic Club!" Tess's delight was quite genuine. Stonewall, now shuttered, was a storied place in the history of Baltimore—and the Monaghan family. She remembered riding her tricycle there. More correctly, she remembered being told that she had ridden her tricycle there. In her memory, it was a land of knees and cigarette smoke and impenetrable grown-up talk, which she tolerated because Harry "Soft Shoes" McGuirk himself, the b'hoy of b'hoys—a b'hoy being the man who gave muldoons their marching orders—would take pity on the restless child and buy her a Coke.

"How did you come to own this?" she asked, as amazed as if her father had procured a Picasso. Tess collected Baltimorebilia, although she was in denial about it. Her office held the neon "It's Time for a Haircut" clock from a Woodlawn barbershop, and she kept her spare change in a miniature model of a Baltimore Gas & Electric truck. She had even begun to acquire old grease tins from the sausage company, Esskay, that had lent its name to her racing greyhound.

The sane one, as she now thought of Esskay. The greyhound had once been her problem child, but everything was relative.

"We need to adhere to a strict don't-ask-don't-tell policy on that issue," her father said. "That way you'll have plausible deniability." Adding, at his only child's shocked expression: "It was just sitting there, for the longest time. What was I supposed to do?"

"Walk on by?" But Tess knew she wouldn't have, either. "I'm so glad you . . . availed yourself of it. After all, you and Mother met there."

"What?" He was genuinely puzzled. "Who told you that?"

"I don't know. Mom? Aunt Kitty? The campaign of 'sixty-six, right? You both worked for the Democratic candidate."

"We worked on the primary campaign of Carlton Sickles, yes. But that's not where we met. We met at the Westview Drive-in the year before. I'm not good on dates, but it was coolish. She wore a lemon-yellow cardigan, only it was pinned to her shoulders with this little chain, with butterflies on either end."

He fluttered his hands along his collarbone, trying to evoke the singular magic of it all. A sweater, moored by butterflies! He made it sound as if Judith Weinstein, as she would have been known then, had been dressed by a coterie of talking woodland creatures, like some princess in a Disney film.

"Are you saying you fell in love at first sight?" This did not fit with what Tess thought she knew of her pragmatic, down-to-earth parents. Love at first sight was for passionate kids. But then—her parents were kids at the time.

"I bird-dogged her," her father said proudly. "Snaked her away from her date. Not that night, but later. She was really interested in politics—your uncle Donald had worked on the Kennedy campaign in 'sixty, was recruiting volunteers for the city council races, so, yeah, it must have been spring 'sixty-five—so I pretended to care, too."

"*Pretended* to care?" Tess was scandalized. Her father's political life had defined him, as far as she knew.

"Oh, eventually I did get caught up with it, but that was more Donald's influence. That night I met your mother, I just wanted to find a way to keep her talking to me. So I told her, yeah, I'd love to volunteer, stuff envelopes, knock on doors, do whatever I could. I figured that would get me more time with her." His fair skin flushed with the memory. "What a way to go."

"Politics?"

"The movie that night. It was *What a Way to Go!* With Shirley MacLaine. I always liked her. We almost named you Shirley."

What's in a name? Only everything. Tess tried to imagine the life and times of Shirley Monaghan. Who were the famous Shirleys? Shirley MacLaine, Shirley Jones, and—oh God, Shirley Booth. Shirley was Noel Airman's code, in *Marjorie Morningstar,* for the first generation of Jewish American Princesses. All things considered, she was happy to be Theresa Esther, mouthful though that was.

"I don't think I've ever seen it."

"Oh, it's great," her father said. "Actually, I watched it on television a couple of years ago, and it didn't hold up so good. But I still love it. Shirley MacLaine is this woman who wants to marry for love, see? And her mother is pushing her to marry the local rich guy, played by Dean Martin. Remember Dean Martin?"

"Yes, there's a channel on cable that appears to be devoted to selling his show on DVD." These were the kinds of things one learned on bed rest.

"Anyway, she marries Dick Van Dyke. But he becomes obsessed with getting rich, showing Dean Martin that he has a real work ethic, and he drops dead of a heart attack, leaving her a wealthy widow. Then she marries Paul Newman, a starving artist who ends up getting rich and being strangled by his own painting machines—"

"Painting machines?"

"Yeah, they paint in time to music. Also there was a monkey."

Also, there was a monkey. This struck Tess as the most trenchant bit of film criticism that she had ever heard from her father, something that could equal Andrew Sarris's auteur theory. She would run this past Lloyd, the film student, the Tess Monaghan theory of awfulness in movies, summed up by one line: *Also, there was a monkey.*

"Then she tries to change her luck by marrying a rich guy, Robert Mitchum—did you know he hit on your aunt Kitty, when she was all of fourteen, one summer at Ocean City?"

Wake up, Tess said in her head, experimentally. It was something she did when her dreams were disturbing, or simply too weird. *Wake up!* Apparently she was conscious.

"But he gets kicked in the head by a bull, when he tries to milk him—he's drunk, you see—so she marries Gene Kelly and he gets, I think, literally torn apart by his fans, so that's where she is when she goes to the psychiatrist and he walks in and, bam, she finds love at last."

"With the psychiatrist?"

"Dean Martin. He's the janitor."

Tess phrased her next question carefully. "And you liked this movie?"

"Honey, it's the movie I saw the night I met your mother. If it had been one of those Annette Funicello movies, or one of those gory movies by, you know, that guy—"

"Herschell Gordon Lewis?" she ventured.

"Or *Mary Poppins*, anything. It could have been a two-hour test pattern and I would think it was the greatest movie ever, because I was sitting in the back-seat of a Dodge Rambler, stealing looks at this girl. She ate popcorn so dainty. She never dropped a piece. Everyone—I mean even the Queen of England—drops a kernel or two. My date that night dropped a lot, ended up with hulls in her teeth. Not your mother."

"Marriages have been made on less," Tess said, meaning it. Still, it bothered her that she had been walking around—back when she was allowed to walk—believing that she was formed in the crucible of local politics, a legacy of the Stonewall Club. *What a Way to Go!* at the Westview Drive-in was a bit of a comedown. "You did go to Stonewall, right? You pretended to be interested in politics to snag Mom, and the lie became true."

"The lie became true," her father agreed, "although we would have been meeting over on the East Side then. That was Donald's turf, in the day. We worked on the primary. We didn't have the heart to campaign after Sickes lost to that nut job Mahoney in the primary. And Maryland ended up sending Agnew to the State House." Her father looked sadder than he did when he thought about the Colts leaving Baltimore, and Tess had always assumed that was the nadir of his adult life. "That was a bad year, 'sixty-six."

"Because your candidate didn't get the nomination?" Tess asked.

"Because we believed in something and we lost. We were young. Kennedy's assassination had been hard on us, but we were teenagers, then. In 'sixty-six, we still thought if you worked for the right guy, you won. Then Mahoney, that kook, that every-home-a-castle guy, got the nomination, and it all fell apart. I didn't vote in the general in 'sixty-six. Then in 'sixty-eight, Bobby Kennedy was killed. The fact is . . ." His voice trailed off.

"Dad?"

"I didn't vote for almost forty years, not until 2004."

Tess could not have been more scandalized if her father had confessed an addiction, or even an affair.

"You were an active member of the party. You did get-out-the-vote. For all I know, you distributed walk-around money."

"There was no walk-around money," her father said, the denial still automatic after all these years. "Besides, none of that stuff means I had to vote."

"So in 2000, 2002—"

"It's not like there's a lot of suspense, electoral collegewise, with Maryland. I campaigned for KKT, in 2002." Tess recognized the shorthand for Kathleen Kennedy Townsend, who had run unsuccessfully for governor. "She sang show tunes on the bus. *Oklahoma!* Let me tell you, *that* was a labor of love. And she lost. First Republican in the State House since Agnew in 'sixty-six. But that one, the 2002 race, didn't hurt. I was old then. Older, at any rate. Too old to get my heart broken, because I didn't put my heart in it anymore."

Her father, ready to leave, first emptied Dempsey's bedpan, then asked where she wanted the Stonewall sign. Tess said it was better suited to her office, where it could share the wall with her neon "Time for a Haircut" clock. He patted her shoulder, uneasy around her belly, then left her to absorb all that she had learned. Her parents had met not at the Stonewall Club, but a local drive-in, while Shirley MacLaine tried to find love. Also, there was a monkey. Her father, who had always teased her mother about her coordinated outfits, remembered exactly what Judith wore that night, down to the butterfly chain securing the lemon-yellow cardigan at her shoulders, while nary a kernel of popcorn fell, or got stuck in her teeth. Had her very existence relied on that detail? She had seen her mother eat popcorn, and did not recall it as an extraordinary feat.

And Tess had almost been Shirley. Could a name change one's destiny? She could not imagine Shirley Monaghan sitting here, with a problematic pregnancy and an even more problematic dog, who was gnawing on something in his crate, possibly his own leg. Shirley Monaghan would probably be knitting booties right now, or making her in-utero progeny listen to Mozart.

Tess Monaghan, by contrast, was trying to figure out how to have another go at the man she now thought of as the Bluebeard of Blythewood Road.

Chapter 8

Giving away money was not as much fun as it used to be, Whitney Talbot decided, sitting at her desk and frowning at her in-box.

The job had been a blast when she started, four years ago. Who wouldn't like being Lady Largesse, as she had thought of herself, dispensing cash to worthy people and their causes. Plus, she was the boss, a role to which she was temperamentally suited. Really, it was amazing she had ever managed to work for anyone. At the family foundation, the only person to whom Whitney answered was her mother, and she had bent that poor woman to her will long ago. She was the chief, the gatekeeper to millions, someone who funded solutions—and yet she found herself in a perpetually bad mood as of late.

Part of the problem was a paradox inherent in philanthropy. When the economy tanked, the demands grew, even as the principal shrank. The guilt engendered by the exponentially multiplying "Nos!" squeezed satisfaction from a now scarce crop of yesses. Just today a woman had pitched an interesting idea about trying to help the city's poorest households use the local farmers markets. The earnest young woman had thought about her plan, deciding it wasn't enough to provide transportation and ensure that more stands took WIC vouchers and food stamps. Poor women from East and West Baltimore needed to be taught how to prepare the foods they were likely to find, how to let the seasons guide what they put on the table, a big adjustment for rich and poor in today's instant-gratification world.

"Once they learn to eat things like squash, eggplant, and kale, that will create support for our next phase, mass community gardens in which they raised their own vegetables," the woman said.

"Kale?" Whitney had echoed, wrinkling her nose.

"It's your bowels' best friend."

"I don't think that's the way we want to sell this," Whitney said. She took stock of her applicant. The woman was wearing a fitted suit, one that must have been custom-tailored to provide such a perfect fit, and quite striking shoes—oxfords with killer heels. Her résumé showed an interesting combination of ivory tower academic work and hands-on restaurant experience. Yet Whitney didn't like her.

Sandwiches arrived and the woman regarded hers skeptically, pulling apart the bread and even sniffing the mayonnaise.

"I never eat tomatoes this late in October," she said. "They're almost certainly shipped from Florida, or Mexico. And are you sure this bread is whole grain? The term is used quite loosely, I've found."

Whitney decided then not to take the project to her board. It was a good idea, but the woman's attitude was all wrong. For the people she was trying to serve, a slice of tomato, whatever its origins, would be an improvement over lake trout, chicken boxes, and fries. Kale, eggplant—those would be a hard sell. Even whole wheat bread was viewed with distaste and suspicion in Baltimore's poor neighborhoods. Whitney had spent enough time in local soup kitchens to familiarize herself with the kitchens' day-to-day needs, and she knew that most diners refused to touch even the heel of a loaf of white bread. This self-important young woman was too rigid to achieve what she wanted. *Sorry, kettle,* she wanted to say, *this pot thinks you have the right plan, but the wrong temperament.*

Instead, she rushed through the lunch and told her she would be in touch, then spent the better part of an hour on the phone with an emergency homeless shelter that always seemed to be reeling from crisis to crisis. "You have to develop some kind of long-term financial plan," Whitney urged, not for the first time, playing ant to the director's harried grasshopper. "Every year, donations drop off in summer, and every autumn you act surprised. I'm sorry that your hot-water heater broke, but we're not a checking account. We want to develop programs, not fund capital expenses."

The director—portrayed in the local media as a saint who cared nothing for herself—cursed Whitney with admirable creativity, managing to invoke her mother, skin tone, and even the contours of her rear end, which did run to flatness. Ah well, one nice thing about cell phones was that they couldn't be slammed down, merely closed with a click.

Truth was, this was a better day than most. The real problem was that she was bored. And she wasn't a very good sport about being bored, which might explain why she had attended two colleges, then raced through three jobs before settling in at the foundation, barely in her thirties at the time. She had so loved being Lady Largesse. She didn't think such things ever got old. But they did. Everything did.

Hmmmm, perhaps that was Don Epstein's problem as well. Beautiful woman after beautiful woman. Only his wives didn't get old, come to think of it. Not a one had made it past forty so far.

She had to admit, Tess seemed to be onto something, even if the rest of the world had moved on, unable to sustain interest when the other celery-green shoe failed to drop. As Sherlock Holmes had said to Watson, to lose one wife was tragic, two was careless, and three—well, Holmes hadn't had a word for that, as Whitney recalled. Of course, she was Watson to Tess's Holmes, if not as fatuously admiring of her friend. Besides, this Watson had a little more mobility than her Holmes just now, and a few ideas of her own about how to track down someone who might kick up a fuss over the missing Carole Epstein. That was what they needed, right? Someone who was willing to make some noise.

She dialed the foundation's sole full-time employee, the much put-upon Marjorie.

"Marjorie—" she began in a wheedling tone.

"Don't give me anything else, I can barely keep up with what I've got," Marjorie snapped. At the foundation for twenty years, she had come to think of its funds as *her* money, with Whitney a cheeky interloper.

"Just one *little* thing. I'd like a quick background check on one of the women who visited me today, Carole Epstein."

"I know your calendar and I watch the news. This isn't foundation business."

"It could be. We've worked with abused women, have we not?"

Marjorie sighed. "Do you have her Social?"

"No, but I have her last two addresses." Quickly, she plugged Don Epstein into Switchboard.com, where his information still carried the Gibson Island address. She read that aloud, adding the Blythewood one from memory. "It's her work history I really want. Try the name Carole Massinger as well. That's her maiden name."

The world was full of loners, as Whitney well knew, being one herself. But it was hard for even a loner to get through life without acquiring a friend or two. Proximity was an interesting phenomenon. Put two people close together, over time, and they would form a bond. She and Tess had become lifelong friends through the random lottery of the housing system at Washington College. Carole Epstein must have held a real job at some point. Her sister had died a decade ago; Carole was married to Don Epstein for less than eighteen months. She hadn't been supporting herself as a handbag designer for all that time.

As it turned out, she had spent at least part of the time selling handbags at Nordstrom, according to Marjorie, quitting only a few months before she married Epstein.

"I'm going to the mall," Whitney announced. "Foundation business."

"Nice work if you can get it," Marjorie groused. "Bring me a smoothie, if you remember. After all, I don't get to bolting out on a whim."

Whitney was the kind of person who attracted sales ladies. Funny, as she was actually rather cheap, in the WASP tradition, and would never dream of paying the prices demanded by today's handbags. Three hundred dollars, five hundred dollars. A thousand dollars! In Baltimore, yet. She got her handbags for free, raiding her mother's closet and grabbing the least frou-frou items. On her last foray, she had taken a Hermès Bolide, and the sharp-eyed saleswomen in Nordstrom circled her hungrily, sure that a woman who carried such a purse was juicy quarry indeed.

Whitney allowed their advances, letting first this one and that one approach. After sizing them up for the better part of an hour, she settled on the most determined clerk, a plump-cheeked little beauty who didn't seem to hear the word "No." Although young, she was quite the breezy pro.

"How long have you worked here?" she asked, examining a Marc Jacobs bag known as the "Patchwork Gennifer." The "Gennifer" was unforgivable, the $1,500 price tag unfathomable.

"Three years," the saleswoman said, substituting a slightly less flamboyant Burberry bag, which Whitney could *almost* imagine carrying—if the decimal point moved one column to the left. Give the woman props: She was like the mother of a young child, quick to distract her charge from an unpleasant sensation by substituting another. *Don't want the lolly? Here's a binky.*

"So you knew Carole Epstein?" A blank look, another quick bag substitution. Kate Spade this time. Warmer, Whitney thought. Warmer.

"Perhaps you knew her as Carole Massinger?"

"Oh, yeah," the woman said, and there was some kind of emotion to it, but Whitney wasn't sure she could identify it. "Kiki. Did she use to wait on you? Because she is *gone*."

It was unclear if the woman knew just how gone Carole was. But she must. Although the story had lost its momentum, it dominated the local media for a week or so.

"How does Carole become Kiki?"

A shrug, another bag sliding down Whitney's arm, another bag sliding up. Dooney & Bourke. "I don't know. She asked to be called Kiki one day. No skin off my—do you like metallics?"

"No," Whitney said. "Was she a friend?"

"I liked her, but, you know."

Whitney chose to translate this sentiment as: *We worked together, we were friendly, I wasn't her bridesmaid.* Bridesmaids! Carole might have been Don Epstein's third wife, but he was her first husband. Had she gone whole hog on the wedding? That could lead to friends, distant family. Whitney made a note to ask Tess if the marriage license indicated a proper church wedding or a courthouse quickie.

"Have you been in touch with her since she left—" Whitney stole a look at the woman's name tag. "—Denise?"

"She came in once." Denise held up a Gucci bag, covered with the signature design of interlocking G's. Whitney shook her head. If a designer wanted to advertise on her body, he could pay for the privilege. "After she got married. She looked at a lot of bags, but she didn't buy anything. I think she was enjoying being on the other side of the counter."

"Did she ever talk about her fiancé before they got married, when you were still working together?"

"Yeah." Denise surrendered, stopped pulling out things to show Whitney. "She said—wait, it was funny what she said, I remember that much. She said . . . 'I've had my sights on him for a long time.' "

"What did she mean by that?"

Denise shrugged. "I thought she meant he was rich, her ticket out."

"She didn't mention that she had known him a long time, or that he had once dated her sister?"

"No, I would have remembered *that.* Or at least the sister part. When she came back in here that one time, she was kinda depressed. Really well dressed, in this amazing coat—"

"A green raincoat?" Whitney had heard Tess describe Carole Esptein often enough to imagine the woman herself, although she had never seen her, except in that one odd photo captured from the Internet. She thought it must be the only photo of Carole, for it was the one all the television shows used when they interviewed Epstein.

"Yes, exactly. She was trying to match a purse to it, in fact. A big purse, which surprised me, because this was last spring—remember how cool and rainy it was—and the trend was going toward small. Carole was usually on top of that kind of stuff, you know? But she didn't buy anything, anyway. She seemed really down. And when I asked her how married life was, she said it wasn't what she expected."

"How so?"

"I don't remember specifics. I just thought it was the usual letdown. All my girlfriends go through it."

It was a good explanation, as good as any for a young bride's down mood on a rainy spring day, and Denise did seem to have a feel for people. Or women. Unlike Freud, she wasn't puzzled about what women wanted. They wanted handbags, and maybe shoes to match. If Whitney were a real shopper, Denise probably could have found the right bag for her. She had been getting closer, stylewise, with each guess.

Whitney put the timeline together in her head. Carole Massinger had known Don Epstein for at least fifteen years, and stayed close enough to him to attend his second wedding. But their romantic relationship had been relatively brief—assuming it hadn't begun as an affair. Who had set their sights on whom? Could it be that Carole Massinger was the first person to glimpse the Bluebeard in Don Epstein, that she had always suspected him in her sister's death and resolved to avenge it somehow? Could she have married him just to get the goods on him? A wife can't be *forced* to testify against her husband, but she can volunteer to do so. Had Carole Massinger rummaged through the rooms of Don Epstein's house, literally and figuratively, defied his orders and found the equivalent of a locked room, in which all his secrets were revealed? Had her foray into Stony Run Park that day been the modern-day equivalent of a call to Sister Ann, summoning help?

"Thank you for your time today," she told Denise.

"You're not going to buy anything, are you?" She sighed. "Frankly, if I had a Hermès like that one, I don't think I'd buy anything, either. If I had a Hermès like that, I think I'd just walk around naked in my house with it, take it to bed with me."

Whitney wondered if purse fetishism was yet another new sexual perversion gaining ground through the power of the Internet.

"I do have a friend who's going to need a diaper bag," she said. "Problem is, she's not the diaper bag sort. In fact, she needs kind of a combination diaper bag/briefcase, with pockets for two cell phones, her gun, and maybe a set of lock picks."

"I have just the thing," Denise said, not the least bit fazed by the mention of a gun. She truly was a pro.

Chapter 9

"A pink diaper bag?" Tess asked in bewilderment, lifting the item from the silver Nordstrom box.

"Pink *and* brown." Whitney took the bag from Tess and began showing her the various pockets. Her over-the-top gestures were uncannily like those used by *The Price Is Right* models, only Whitney got to do all the talking on her game show. "Your cell can go here, and in a pinch I think you could wrap your Beretta in the portable changing pad. Check out the antique brass tone stroller clips. And it converts to a knapsack."

She demonstrated, marching up and down, pretending to push a stroller and walk a dog.

"Okay, I like the last feature, but it's still pink and"—Tess looked at the label—"made by someone called Petunia Pickle Bottom. Also, did I mention? It's *pink*." She couldn't bear to go into the harangue about the evil eye, and how she didn't want any baby gifts until there was, in fact, a baby. The concept of a baby was still strangely abstract to Tess. She was eight weeks away from the delivery date, and despite the constant signs of life within her—Fifi La Pew was a big kicker, go figure—seemed to have zero maternal instincts. She wasn't even sure she believed there was a child in her. She would not be surprised to discover that the object in her belly was an enormous . . . radish. That was, in fact, a recent dream. She'd given birth to a radish, and everyone said it looked just like her.

"I wasn't being a sexist," Whitney said. "It just has the best configuration of pockets. I also like that combination of pink and brown. Makes me think of Baskin-Robbins. Besides, it's not for you, it's for the baby."

"I don't know much about motherhood," Tess admitted. "But I'm pretty sure the diaper bag is, in fact, for me. For me and Crow, who will probably *like* changing diapers. Who will probably be such a good parent that I will be largely irrelevant."

"Are you going to be competitive about parenting, too?" Whitney asked.

"I'm not." But Tess didn't have the energy to deny something that was so clearly true. "I'm just feeling inadequate. Crow bustles around, happy and confident, without a single care in the world, whereas I'm stuck in chronic worry mode."

"Well, I have another gift that might cheer you up."

"Is it alcohol? Her brain must be more or less developed by now. Besides, IQ is highly overrated. Look at you. Near genius IQ, but your taste is crap."

"This is better than alcohol." Whitney, who had continued to pace the room, modeling the diaper bag, stopped and posed dramatically, arms akimbo. "Ethel Zimmerman!"

Tess waited, thinking there must be more, but Whitney just stood there, pleased to the point of smugness.

"I'm afraid I already know Ethel Merman's real name, but thanks for the trivia. Did you know that Jacqueline Susann was the one who told her what to say, when people asked why she changed it? Something about how people would pass out from the heat if 'Zimmerman' were up in lights."

"And she was married to Ernest Borgnine for thirty-two days, a fact immortalized by a Chapter in her autobiography—a single blank page," Whitney said.

Sheesh, Tess thought, *who's the competitive one here?*

"However, this is a different Ethel Zimmerman. Lives in Severna Park, a longtime neighbor of the

Massingers. She was Carole's in-case-of-emergency person at Nordstrom. What do you want to bet she's also the person Carole called the weekend she couldn't raise her sister on the phone?"

"Hence, my diaper bag?" Tess was torn between admiration and envy. It was galling, being trapped here, while Whitney was free to follow up hunches, roam the world, make things happen.

"You can't imagine the half of it," Whitney said. "Do you know anyone who wants a Marc Jacobs wallet?"

"Have you visited Ethel yet? Chatted her up?"

Whitney shook her head. "I thought about it. But I really think she needs to come see you, have you explain what you think happened, and why. Even if you only saw Carole through your window, you have a connection to her that I can't quite match. She's *real* to you. To me, she's just a puzzle."

"How are we going to get some woman from Severna Park to come up here and talk to me?"

"Well, there's light rail, if she doesn't drive—"

"No, I mean, what can I say that would persuade her that this can't be done over the phone, that I need to meet her face-to-face?"

Whitney was nonplussed. In that most unusual silence, the sounds of Dempsey's chewing filled the room. He had progressed from trying to eat his own leg to gnawing on the bars on his crate. The dog's behavior had improved, but only with Tess. He was still generally hateful to everyone else, and had to be crated when anyone but Crow was in the house. And Lloyd refused to walk him with the other dogs, as it always ended in a melee.

So, during the day, when Dempsey needed to take bathroom breaks, Tess used an antique cane—another bizarre gift from her aunt, who seemed to confuse her pregnancy with some sort of Victorian-era malady—to lift the crate's lock and swing the door open. He trotted outside, did his business, went mano a mano with the invisible fencing for a few rounds, then returned docilely to his crate. He wouldn't go out in the dark, however; released in the middle of the night, he still used her chamber pot. He was scared of the dark. It was the only sign of weakness in the dog, who seemed to be girding himself for some epic battle. Now, as his teeth grated against the metal, Tess couldn't help wondering if he was sharpening them in preparation for his next meeting with Don Epstein, or whatever hired gun had taken away the dog's beloved mistress.

"Dempsey!" she said. "We can ask Mrs. Zimmerman if she'll come up here to see Dempsey, consider taking him in as a favor to Carole."

"She won't," Whitney said. "Unless she's crazy."

"And I wouldn't wish him on her. But that would be enough to get her here, and let me lay out my ideas about what really happened to Carole. We'll call her, say that Carole left something in our care and that we have instructions to turn it over to her. But what do you think we'll gain by talking to Ethel face-to-face?"

"You are really getting slow. Are you sure *your* brain function is okay? She's Carole's in-case-of-emergency person. Here's our emergency."

"I think that applies more to workplace accidents," Tess said. "But, okay, I get it. She can turn up the heat, put forward a sympathetic version of Carole in opposition to the bitch-stole-my-money portrait that Epstein has painted. You are pretty smart. Taste in diaper bags aside."

"Trust me, I picked the best one."

Ethel Zimmerman sounded extremely frail on the phone, an elderly woman with a hoarse, wispy voice that Tess could barely hear. Still, she didn't hesitate when asked if she would come to Baltimore to talk about Carole; Tess didn't even need to dangle the bait of Dempsey. Mrs. Zimmerman did ask if their meeting could wait until the next afternoon—she confessed that she found traffic terrifying after four o'clock—

and Tess, her heart full of sympathy for the older woman, said that it could.

The next day, Crow cleaned up the house before leaving for work, then made sure the door was unlocked so Tess wouldn't make an unnecessary trip to the door. At noon—a full hour before Mrs. Zimmerman was expected—a sharp knock sounded, and Tess yelled, "Come in, I'm in the back."

But could this be Mrs. Zimmerman? Tess's guest—*guests*—were two forty-something woman with hard athletic builds and almost identical chin-length bobs. At first glance they appeared to be sisters. At second, Tess realized they simply had remarkably similar taste.

"Mrs. Zimmerman?"

The two women exchanged a look. "No, we're—I'm Beth Angleton—"

"And I'm Liz Matthias."

They looked at Tess expectantly, as if their names should explain everything.

"Um—"

"We're May's parents? Lloyd's girlfriend?" Their level gazes, while not exactly judgmental, managed to convey that they would know *instantly* who Tess Monaghan was, if she had shown up, unannounced, at their home. *I have preeclampsia*, Tess wanted to say.

I'm in the middle of a possible murder investigation, I'm a little distracted.

"Of course. Did Lloyd say you would be coming by? We've been—well, life—as you can see—" She indicated her bed, the dog, the room, her mound of a belly in hopes that these things would sum up the insanity that was her life. Thank God, Crow had cleaned the house and the chamber pot was empty.

"No, we didn't tell Lloyd we were coming to meet with you," said Beth. Or was it Liz? Were they both actually Elizabeth? Had they been forced to differentiate their nicknames to avoid confusion? "This is awkward, but—we're really not happy with Lloyd as a companion for May."

On her best day, Tess could come up with a dozen reasons why Lloyd wasn't a fit companion for anyone. But that was her prerogative. How dare these oh-so-perfect, put-together mommies—they also wore complementary silver earrings and stunning designer glasses—imply that Lloyd wasn't the right boyfriend for their precious May? She decided to put them on the defensive.

"Are we talking about race?"

"Of course not!" Beth and Liz chorused. Then Beth—or was it Liz?—added: "You can't possibly think *we're* bigoted."

"Why not?" Tess challenged.

"We adopted a girl from China. Our own lives, our choices, have exposed us to—I won't say as much prejudice as someone like Lloyd might have known, but it's certainly made us sensitive to judging people according to external standards. We *love* Lloyd. He's bright, curious. In the beginning, we thought he was a good influence on May."

"So what's your problem?" Tess asked. She didn't mean it to sound quite so peevish and hostile, but—she was pregnant and stuck in this room. People had to grant her a little latitude, and not just on mood. She had to take sponge baths, for example. The highlight of her week was the shower she was allowed to have while sitting on a plastic stool. She got pretty stinky by day six, and this was day five. She dared anyone to be cheerful under such circumstances.

"Surely you know?" asked Beth, who appeared to be the spokeswoman. It wasn't so hard to tell them apart, after all. Beth's eyes were blue, while Liz's tended toward green. "We just assumed—I mean, he said he had gotten it from your, um, partner, so we thought he had been consulted."

Tess liked the fact that one of May's two mommies had to grope for the proper term to describe Crow. She fought down the urge to scream out, Cloris

Leachmanlike, "He *vuz* my boyfriend!" But even if they got the *Young Frankenstein* reference, these terribly earnest women probably wouldn't be amused by it.

"What did he get from Crow? Some inappropriate film?" In a flash, Tess knew what had happened. "Did he screen *In the Realm of the Senses* for May? Or something by Peter Greenaway? You have to understand, to Lloyd, film is film, it's all about technique, not content. I've tried to explain that other people have different sensibilities, but—"

"This isn't about a movie," Beth said.

"Would that it were," Liz muttered.

"Well, *what* then?" Tess snapped. "I don't mean to be impatient, but I am expecting someone this afternoon, and if you could just get down to cases—"

"This past weekend was May's birthday," Beth said. "Lloyd gave her a ring and asked her to marry him."

Tess reached Crow at work, but he was innocent of Lloyd's intentions, as it turned out. He had shown Lloyd the ring, an heirloom from his mother's family, and told him that it would be his one day, when he found the woman he wanted to marry. Crow just hadn't expected "one day" to come so soon.

"You can't even call it stealing," Crow said. "I told him that he could have it when he decided to get married. I'm not glad he took it without asking, but he took it for its rightful purpose, didn't hock it. It's not that long ago that Lloyd might have done just that. That's progress."

"Why would he want to get married?"

"He's in love," Crow said.

"Eighteen-year-old boys fall in love every day. They also fall *out.* However, they don't go out and propose every day. Sort of the opposite."

"We did screen Zeffirelli's *Romeo and Juliet*, alongside Baz Luhrmann's version. I saw it as an opportunity to see how a classic text was interpreted in two different eras, but Lloyd—well, I guess Lloyd was focusing on something else."

"You don't seem as upset about this as you might," Tess said.

"It's not *tragic*," Crow said. "I mean, I don't think it's the best idea he's ever had, but it's hard for me to get upset because a teenage boy, deeply in love with a teenage girl, decided he wanted to marry her."

"Actually, it could turn out to be absolutely tragic," Tess argued. "They could ruin their lives. What if they have a baby? Oh my God, is that it? Is she pregnant?"

Crow laughed. "Truthfully, I'm not even sure they've had sex yet. I let Lloyd have as much privacy as possible on that score. But you've met May, Tess, and heard her ten-year plan for her life—Teach for America, followed by graduate school. She's not going to get knocked up. Look, we'll deal with this, but your anger is really all out of proportion."

A rap on the door, followed by a quavering "Hello?" alerted Tess to the arrival of the guest she had been expecting, Mrs. Zimmerman. She said a hasty goodbye. Why was she so upset? A family heirloom, an engagement ring—didn't *Crow* have any use for it? Were they not to be married then, at some point? Crow was the one who used to press for marriage; she had told him it made no sense unless they had children, thinking all the while—we will *never* have children. But now they were having a child, and she couldn't remember the last time Crow had mentioned marriage. Was he really going to be there for her? Could she rely on him?

She called out to Ethel "not the Merm" Zimmerman, her mind fixated on the ring she had never seen. It was probably ornate, not to her taste. Or small, better suited to someone petite. That was it, right? The *ring* didn't suit her, but she still suited the man. Right? Right?

Chapter 10

Perhaps it was inevitable that Tess Monaghan's favorite girlhood book was *Harriet the Spy.* As a grown-up Harriet, she had not been able to avail herself of many of Harriet's techniques—there were few dumbwaiters in Baltimore into which she could crawl, and a utility belt simply called too much attention to the wearer—but it was Harriet who taught her to love black-and-white composition books. And she had liked Harriet's practice of trying to figure out what people looked like based on simply hearing their voices. After speaking to Ethel Zimmerman on the phone, she decided the wispy-voiced lady would be quite frail, perhaps dependent on a walker, and given to an old-fashioned sense of propriety in dress. A hat, even gloves.

Ah, well—not even Harriet batted 1.000 in this particular game. Ethel Zimmerman, a very peppy seventy-something, all but bounded into Tess's sickroom, arrayed in a bright blue tracksuit and white Pumas. She *was* wearing a hat of sorts—a powder-blue visor stamped with the name of an Atlantic City casino.

"Do you gamble?" Tess asked this vision in peacock blue, stalling while she tried to find her mental footing. She had prepared for a meeting with someone who would need to be coddled. This woman looked like she could arm wrestle Tess and win, even back in her pre-pregnancy days.

"Do I . . . ?" She touched the brim of her visor. "Oh, no. Yard sale. Fifty cents. They wanted a *dollar.*" She plucked the sleeve of her tracksuit. "This still had the tags on it. Fifty-five dollars, if you can believe it. I got it for seven on eBay."

"And the shoes?"

"Shoes are tough," Mrs. Zimmerman admitted in her thin whisper. "I go to DSW, places like that. I won't wear used shoes. Or underwear. I'm fussy that way."

She said this with pride, as if this principle made her unusual, even finicky.

"Is there something wrong?" Mrs. Zimmerman asked.

"Oh, no, it's just that—you're so much . . . *bouncier* than I expected. On the phone you sounded . . ." There was simply no euphemism for *old and frail*, so Tess let the sentence go.

"Cancer of the larynx," she said with amazing cheer. "My husband left while I was still in the hospital. Best thing that ever happened to me, that partial laryngectomy, because otherwise I might not have had a Ralphectomy, and that's what needed cut out of my life."

Wow, Tess thought. And people think oversharing is a phenomenon limited to the young.

"So you knew Carole," Ethel said, drawing up a chair. "And she asked you to get in touch with me?"

"Sort of," Tess said. "It's complicated. First—if you don't mind—could you tell me how well you knew her, if you kept in touch with her through the years?"

"I've known her all her life. Her sister, too. Our neighborhood may not be a fancy one, but it was stable. Her older sister was good friends with my sons. Carole was younger, one of those change-of-life babies, we called them then, back when people didn't wait, and start trying to have babies at forty." She gave Tess's belly a significant look.

"I'm thirty-five," Tess said faintly, wondering if she should add: *And it was an accident! My boyfriend has super sperm! It defeated a diaphragm and spermicide. This is a zygote of destiny.*

"Carole's sister, she was like a daughter to me, and my sons felt the same way about the Massingers. They wore a path between the two houses, coming and going. Carole was so much younger, she was more like a grandchild. We all doted on her, but it only made her sweeter. In fact, she was the best behaved of the lot. People talk about spoiling children as if they are plants that get overwatered and rot at the root. It's actually hard to pay too much attention to a child. A lot of what people call spoiling is ignoring, substituting things for time. These Game Boys, these iPods, all these computers and gadgets—they let the parents off the hook, don't they? There's a difference between buying a child everything under the sun and spending time with them. I stayed home with my boys, and you couldn't ask for nicer kids."

Tess couldn't help inferring a judgment. "My husband and I have the kind of jobs that will allow us to share child care."

Husband? Had she called Crow her husband just to avoid more unsolicited advice from Mrs. Zimmerman? She felt a little stab of what she decided to call heartburn.

Mrs. Zimmerman snorted. "Sure, if you say so. Good luck with that."

"My mother worked," Tess said. "At the National Security Agency."

At least Ethel Zimmerman knew better than to criticize a Baltimore girl's mother. "So did Glenda

Massinger. Out of necessity—they always had trouble making ends meet, the Massingers. That's another reason I was so close to the girls. They would come to my house after school. First Danielle, then Carole, ten years later. Oh, Glenda and Duane worked hard, for all it got them. They died in a car accident."

"Yes, I had heard that."

"And Danielle was left alone with her sister, barely thirteen at the time. She put her own dreams on hold, got a decent job, made sure that Carole wanted for little. Put her social life on hold, too, until Carole was in high school. That's when Don Epstein first started coming around."

"Wasn't he married then?"

Mrs. Zimmerman nodded, lips pursed.

"I tried not to judge," she said. Tess found that hard to believe. "He was her boss, she said they had to work overtime some nights, and I turned a blind eye. The thing is, Danielle was younger and older than her years. Responsible about money. Stupid about men."

"You didn't like Don Epstein?"

Ethel Zimmerman considered this. "No, no—I can't say that. He was courteous, did nice things for Danielle, treated her well. Oh, the presents he started to give her once they started dating officially. Jewelry, fancy clothes. She was dazzled. Too dazzled. I was worried he was toying with her, that he would move on to somebody else more . . . like him."

"More like him?"

"Rich, well-to-do. They tend to stick to their own, rich people." Mrs. Zimmerman studied Tess. "Your *husband*"—she managed to make it sound as if she didn't believe there was one, but perhaps, Tess thought, that was her own hormone-fueled paranoia—"does he have a similar background to yours?"

Tess had never even considered this "We're both only children . . ." But that was the only overlap she could see. Crow's parents had *ancestors*, the kind of families who had arrived in the colonies from England—not on the *Mayflower*, but not far behind. His father was an academic, a professor of economics at the University of Virginia, his mother a sculptor. He had grown up in a bookish, indulgent household, encouraged to speak his mind and follow his bliss.

Her parents, smart as they were, didn't even have college diplomas, and "bliss" was not part of their vocabulary.

"A man can't be happy if he marries below his station," Mrs. Zimmerman warned darkly, as if she could read Tess's mind. "Ralph and I may not have gone the distance, but we made a good run at it. But if you start off unequal, it never balances out. That's what I told Danielle, all those years ago. He was rich, he lived high. She'd never be a good fit."

Tess wondered if Danielle had sought Mrs. Zimmerman's counsel on love and marriage. It probably didn't matter. Tess hadn't, and yet here she was, getting her ear chewed off a mere ten minutes after meeting the woman.

"But Don Epstein's money came mainly from his first wife," Tess said. "The check-cashing businesses belonged to her late father, although Epstein built them up."

"And you see how *that* ended."

Tess was beginning to see why Ralph might have bolted.

"There were conflicting reports, around the time of Danielle's death, that she and Don were engaged. He said no, but her sister seemed to believe he had proposed."

"I think Danielle might have told Carole that to save face, given how long they had been dating by then."

"Did you find her death suspicious?"

"Suspicious? Goodness, no. Sad, yes, but not suspicious. Some families are just a magnet for tragedy. I should have noticed that her car hadn't moved for days, but it was Easter time and I was running around."

"Were you surprised when Carole married him?"

"Actually I didn't know anything about it until I turned on the six o'clock news and found out she had left him, taking most of his money. *That* was quite the shock."

"You weren't in touch then? When did you last speak?"

Mrs. Zimmerman's face clouded over. "We had a little falling out, I'm sorry to say. You see, she didn't finish school, dropped out a month shy of graduation. True, she had lost Danielle the year before and it was a vicious shock. But I told her Danielle would have wanted her to finish, that she had made sacrifices so Carole would have a college degree."

"She stopped speaking to you because you said she should stay in college?" Lifelong quarrels had been based on smaller things, as Tess knew, but it still seemed sad to her. Mrs. Zimmerman might be a know-it-all busybody, but Carole Massinger could have used a buttinsky in her life. That seemed to be another part of Don Epstein's pattern: He preferred women who were alone in the world. She had yet to find anything about his second wife, Annette, and Mary had only her father, who died soon after her marriage.

"Carole could be quite . . . willful. She said she needed to start over, with new memories. She sold the house—got a nice sum for it, too, although she didn't sell anywhere near the height of the market. She sold everything in it. She said the memories were choking her. She was going to use the capital to start a gift-basket business. She did make a good muffin, I have to say. But I'm not sure that's enough to make it in the gift-basket business. Carole was a little impractical."

"She was choking on memories, yet she took up with her sister's ex-boyfriend."

"Not straight off," Mrs. Zimmerman pointed out. "I think she fell into the habit of leaning on Don. They went to a grief counseling group together—that's where Carole met Annette, and the three of them began palling around. She didn't have anyone else. And he, unlike me, didn't try to tell Carole not to do what she had her heart set on doing."

"She told you that?"

"Just an assumption. As I said, we quarreled. It's not so odd, that she would want to marry him, or he would want to marry her. She looks like Danielle. Prettier actually, because she has a real spunky quality. Danielle never got in the habit of standing up for herself."

"So she marries this man whose first wife gets murdered, whose second wife dies in a hospital, whose girlfriend has a freak fall—"

"You shouldn't have such morbid thoughts," Mrs. Zimmerman said. "Your baby will be born warped."

It was hard, just then, not to order the woman out of the house. She was like some creepy old soothsayer, the very evil eye that Tess had been trying to ward off, and she had actually invited Mrs. Zimmerman into her home. But Tess stopped and thought before she spoke, a habit that she had spent a long time cultivating.

"Yet you believe that Carole took his money and ran away, just because he says so?"

Mrs. Zimmerman hesitated. "I don't know," she said. "I don't want to believe that. But computers don't lie, do they?"

"They could be manipulated—especially by someone who owns a chain of check-cashing stores. What do you think, Mrs. Zimmerman, in your gut? Would the girl you knew have done this?"

Mrs. Zimmerman thought. Thinking was not particularly kind to her face, grooved with age as it was. Cigarettes had not been kind to her. One could argue that life hadn't been that kind to her, either. Her husband had left, she had been through surgery and probably chemo and speech therapy. The Massingers weren't the only tragedy magnet on their block in Severna Park.

"Carole never ran away from a fight in her life," she said at last. "Like I said, she had spunk. Danielle was the weak one, rest her soul. She never stood up to anyone."

"And if she came to believe that Don hurt her sister?"

"She would do whatever it took to bring him to justice."

"You should tell the police that. And the newspaper."

"The *Beacon-Light*? Why would they care what some old lady from Severna Park had to say?"

"I think they'd like to talk to anyone who knew Carole, who can sketch a more human portrait of her. After all, her side of the story has never been told."

Tess didn't wait for Mrs. Zimmerman to think about this, but quickly dialed the city editor at the *Beacon-Light*, her sole contact at the newspaper. The "Blight" had been roiled by economic pressures, reducing its staff by more than a third. But Kevin Feeney was a solid journalist, and Tess was delivering him an exclusive, an intimate of Carole Massinger's willing to speak at length. There would be no simple "She was a quiet child" homilies from Mrs. Zimmerman. She would talk. And talk and talk and talk. Primed like a pump, she spoke to a reporter for so long that it was almost dusk by the time she hung up. The dog walkers were beginning to arrive in the park.

"This is how Carole first came to my attention," Tess said. "She and her dog wore matching coats."

"She always did like nice things. When she was thirteen—thirteen, mind you—she got it in her head that she wanted one of those bubble skirts that were so popular. And not just any bubble skirt, but a designer one like Madonna wore. Dulcie and Gabba-Gabba-Hay, I think." It took Tess a moment to translate this to Dolce & Gabbana. "It cost something like four hundred dollars and she wanted to go into her savings account. Her parents talked her out of that, thank goodness. So much money for such an ugly thing."

"Yet now bubble skirts are back," Tess said.

"And Madonna never went away. It just goes to show," Mrs. Zimmerman said. She stood, did a few quick deep knee-bends to loosen her joints, stiff after so many hours of sitting. Then she was off, leaving Tess to wonder: *What did it go to show*? The cyclical nature of fashion, the resilience of a pop star, or the eternal verity of young girls yearning for things they would regret?

Chapter 11

Ethel Zimmerman's in-depth interview with the *Beacon-Light* brought results beyond Tess's wildest dreams. The story was now hot enough for the national crowd. Ethel Zimmerman became the get of gets, holding out for not merely for the *Today* show, but Matt Lauer himself. *Today* even sent a crew to Tess's home to get what they called B-roll of Dempsey, but Dempsey attempted to attack the young woman producer, and it was determined that a still photograph of the dog, held firmly in Tess's arms, would suffice.

The intensity of the media coverage turned the case into a bona fide red ball—stepped-up efforts to determine if Carole's phone could be traced via the GPS device implanted in all cell phones, a sizable award offered by a local bank. From her sun porch, Tess watched men and cadaver dogs search the park.

The one tangible result? Don Epstein, according to the *Beacon-Light*, began receiving literal sacks of mail, most of it from supportive women. Oh, there were some accusatory letters as well, and offers to pray for his mortal soul, but the bulk of the mail was from women angling to be wife number four.

"Why do you think that it is?" an earnest reporter asked Epstein, arranging her features in that ubiquitous serious-yet-furrowless expression. Tess believed it must be taught in the nation's broadcasting schools: Concerned Face 101.

"Most women see that I'm the wounded party here. My wife left me. She took my money. They can search my house and the woods behind my house and all of Baltimore, and they're never going to find her."

"But you must admit, Mr. Epstein—"

"Call me Don." Was he actually flirting?

"You must admit that this all seems rather, well, ironic." If Tess Monaghan weren't seven months pregnant, she would have downed a shot, in honor of a drinking game she and Whitney had devised years ago: Whenever anyone misused the word "ironic," slam back tequila. On a good night it was possible to get drunk fifteen minutes into the six o'clock news.

"Your first two wives are dead. You had a girlfriend, between those two wives, and she died in a fall. That girlfriend happened to be the older sister of your third wife. Can you blame people for being suspicious?"

"Yes," he said, composed and measured. *He must have hired a media coach,* Tess thought. There was no sign of the defensive man that Mrs. Blossom had met. "Yes, I can blame people, and our tabloid culture, with its unquenchable thirst for other people's tragedies."

Definitely a media coach, maybe a high-powered PR firm. There was no way Don Epstein had put that sentence together spontaneously.

"I lost my first wife to a killer who was never caught. My second wife died while in a hospital, but I'm not allowed to discuss the circumstances. A woman who worked for me, a woman I was dating, died in an accident. Can you imagine what that's been like for me?"

"Can you imagine," Tess asked the television, "what that was like for *them*?"

"I'm cutting you off," Crow said. He was unhappy with her, especially since the photo of Dempsey continued to be broadcast with Tess so clearly visible. She thought she should be the one who was upset, given that she had a shiny moon-face to match her planet of a stomach. But Crow had taken Sergeant Lenhardt's warnings to heart. This was a dangerous man. It was better not to provoke him. It wouldn't take a genius to figure out who had pushed Ethel Zimmerman toward the limelight.

"You and your land of counterpane, playing games," Crow had said. Tess didn't know that a reference to Robert Louis Stevenson's *A Child's Garden of Verses* could be so bitter and accusatory.

"I think of myself as Boo Radley, watching quietly, at the ready to avenge."

"You look more like Scout, trapped in her ham costume."

Crow had never said anything so cruel before, but his words were the least of her worries. For while Crow insisted that Lloyd take the ring back from May, it had been placed in a safe deposit box. There was no talk of a ring for Tess, no discussion of marriage. She moped on her chaise longue, thinking about all the deadbeat dads she had followed over the years, all the divorces. When she was flush, and could pick and choose her jobs, divorce work was always the first thing she jettisoned. She preferred Dumpster diving in corporate espionage cases over divorce cases. The slime from the Dumpster came off in the shower.

"How do you envision our future?" she asked Crow now.

"You know I try not to," he said. "People are happier if they live in the moment."

"But you have to plan some things. Look at your job. You book bands months in advance. It's not quite November and you're already planning your Mardi Gras lineup."

"True, but the competition for authentic New Orleans music is fierce that time of year—"

"So you can't go through life without planning."

"Excuse me, aren't you the woman who won't let anyone buy her a crib, or paint a room, until the baby is actually here?"

"Yes, but . . ."

"But?"

If a newscaster were in the room with them, the moment probably would have been described as a pregnant pause. An ironically pregnant pause.

Crow's cell phone began buzzing and he glanced at the caller ID. "Lloyd," he said. "Remember we're having him, May, and May's moms over tomorrow, to talk about this whole engagement thing."

"But he gave the ring back," Tess said. *And you put it in a safe deposit box because you clearly don't think you have any use for it.*

"Getting the ring back was the easy part," Crow said. "The feelings don't just slide off."

"I wonder if Don Epstein always used the same ring? It would have been morbid, I suppose, but what else would you do with them? What's the etiquette? Maybe the ring is cursed. I'm surprised that Don Epstein hasn't floated that theory."

Tess opened her computer, began clicking away again. She looked for photos of Mary Epstein, several of which had run with the *Beacon-Light*'s recent overview of Epstein's checkered marital history. "Look, I think it's the same. Art Deco, some darker stone worked into the setting. Of course that ring was taken at the hospital. Unless Epstein was brazen enough to lie about that? I mean, if he's killing them, he wouldn't be above stealing—"

Crow sighed and carried her tray away.

Tess had been given permission to take an extra shower to prepare for the brunch with Beth and Liz. There wasn't much she could do with her appearance at this point, but she attempted to style her hair, Dempsey growling at the blow dryer throughout the process.

Beth, Liz, and May arrived exactly on time. Lloyd, bless him, was late as usual. *Way to impress your mothers-in-law*, Tess thought. May, bracketed by her mothers, met his eyes only briefly, then returned to staring at her lap. She was an undeniably beautiful girl, with straight hair that hung halfway down her back and a willowy frame. She was quiet, at least in Tess's presence, and it had been hard to imagine how she managed as a tutor, especially with someone as obdurate and contrary as Lloyd. At least, it was difficult to imagine until one saw the way Lloyd looked at her.

After some awkward and superficial conversation about Crow's food—*How could blueberry macadamia nut muffins be low-fat?*—Beth finally got down to cases.

"Lloyd, we're not going to forbid you to see May, because I think that would be counterproductive," she said. "But the idea of being engaged at your age is simply ridiculous."

Tess worried that Lloyd would get angry, revert to the posturing swagger he had used when she first knew him. But Lloyd was remarkably composed.

"Why?" he asked.

The question seemed to catch Beth off-guard, perhaps because she considered the reasons so obvious. Tess had, too—until Lloyd asked that they be enumerated. Why shouldn't people get engaged at eighteen? *They were too young. It wouldn't work out. They might compromise their futures. They couldn't possibly know what they wanted. What was the rush?*

Tess knew all these things were true, yet they sounded a little hollow, racing through her head. Her parents hadn't been that much older.

"You're too young," Beth began.

"Romeo and Juliet were teenagers," Lloyd said.

"Yes—in a play," Beth said. "A play about people whose life expectancy was about half yours, in an era where people made early marriages, in part, because—" She broke off, clearly not wanting to finish her thought. Tess wondered if she had caught herself before suggesting that people used to get married in order to have sex. Funny, how they continued to tiptoe around that topic.

"Would you and Liz get married, if you could?" Lloyd asked.

"That's not relevant to this discussion," Beth said, even as Liz said, "We might, if *some* people would consider going to California."

"I'm not spending the money to go all the way to California to go through some patriarchal ceremony that doesn't, in the end, mean anything."

"It would mean something to *me*," Liz said.

May sat between them, eyes downcast. Tess tried to imagine the world as this girl saw it. Did she remember the orphanage where she had lived until she was almost three? Did she dream about the parents who had abandoned her, wonder about a world where the mere fact of gender could make a child unwanted? What had she thought about going from no mother to two? When had it registered that her life was not like most children's? What had drawn her to Lloyd? Did they talk about their lives, their childhoods? Did she feel luckier by contrast, knowing that Lloyd's biological mother had essentially abandoned him at his stepfather's request?

"What about you, May?" Tess asked.

"I love Lloyd," she said. "Beth and Liz say I can't know that. But I do."

"Actually, I was wondering where you stood on their marriage?"

Beth flushed, angry. Tess knew she had overstepped, but she didn't care.

"I want them to be happy," May said.

"We are happy," Beth and Liz chorused.

"You were," their daughter said. "Before this summer, when Liz started to talk about getting married. Then you started to fight. A lot."

"But we're not fighting about our commitment to one another," Beth said. "We're fighting about a principle. To me, marriage is an institution from which I was barred for most of my adult life. Like . . . a country club that didn't take blacks or Jews. Sorry, Lloyd."

"No problem," he said. "I know I'm black."

That sparked some weak chuckles, undercutting the tension in the room. Beth continued: "The thing is, when a place that has banned you changes the rules because of external pressure, that doesn't mean you rush to join."

"You just didn't want to sign a prenup," Liz said.

"Liz! That's not fair, not fair at all."

Tess, who had watched far more daytime television in the past month than she had seen in her previous thirty-five years, began to feel as if she were in the middle of her own bizarre talk show.

"We're not here to talk about our relationship," Beth said.

"Why not?" May asked. "You've been telling me what I can do. Why can't I have an opinion about what you do?"

"Do you?" Crow asked. "What do you want, May?"

The question seemed to catch her off-guard. Had no one ever asked her this? Her two mothers waited, as if May were an oracle, as if she had the power to control their future. She did, Tess realized, and not just in the matter of marriage. She was their child, their lives were in thrall to her.

"I want you to be happy," she said. "But you're both so determined to win that it's become impossible. It's the same with Lloyd and me, only you agree on that.

You're so fixated on winning the argument that you've never bothered to think about why I took the ring, why I might want to marry Lloyd."

"You're too young," Beth began again.

May rolled her eyes and sighed exaggeratedly, which didn't exactly refute Beth's point.

"Your brain isn't even fully formed," Liz put in. "Teenagers don't have the same brain chemistry as adults. You're not using your frontal lobe to make decisions. I heard it on NPR!"

Crow caught Tess's eye at that moment, which was disastrous. She began to laugh, then cough, then laugh *and* cough. It was the combination of "frontal lobe" with the PC battle cry, "I heard it on NPR!" She laughed so hard that Dempsey began barking, almost as if joining in. It was infectious, catching May, then Lloyd and Crow, Beth, and finally, reluctantly, Liz.

"Okay, okay," Beth said at last. "Why do you want to marry Lloyd?"

"I'm not sure I do," May said, and the look on Lloyd's face almost shattered Tess's heart. "But that's part of being engaged, right? You make a commitment to get married, but you have time to think about it."

"May?" Crow said. "At the risk of piling on more advice, I have to say that engagement isn't something you do as a trial. You get engaged when you're *sure* of what you want." Tess's heart lurched on her own behalf. Was this why Crow no longer spoke of marrying her? "I believe you love Lloyd and he loves you. But he proposed precisely because he knows you're not one hundred percent sure of him. He was trying to bind you to him prematurely. Just be in love, don't worry about putting names to it."

"That's part of it," May admitted. "But the thing I can't forget is that Beth and Liz met when they weren't much older than we are now, back in college. They let ten years go by before they were together."

"In part," Beth said dryly, "because Liz married a man first."

"I didn't get a wedding then, either. Is it so wrong to want one wedding in a lifetime?"

"But don't you wish you had those ten years?" May asked. "Don't you regret doubting yourselves, being skeptical of what you felt?"

The two women exchanged a glance.

"I do," Liz said.

"I do, too," Beth said.

"Well," Lloyd said. "That's a kind of wedding right there, ain't it?"

Beth and Liz had no problem laughing at themselves this time. They weren't humorless, as Tess had first thought. Just worried about their daughter.

Beth plucked a carrot curl from the salad and placed it on Liz's finger.

"Marriage in Massachusetts, not California," she said. "Party here. Friends and family, nothing too crazy."

Tess looked at the carrot curl and thought about the Art Deco behemoth that Epstein had used for two wives. Where was it now? What if Carole had found it in his effects? What would that signify? The ring mattered, she was sure of it. No, not that ring. Carole had found something else in Don Epstein's house, the importance of which only she understood.

Then Tess realized she had confused the plot of *Rear Window* with her own life.

Chapter 12

Tess kept clicking back and forth, back and forth, looking at the ring on first Mary Epstein's hand, then Annette's. It had to be the same ring. Then again, maybe it was cheaper than it looked, and he had a whole drawer full of them, encased in plastic globes, gumball machine ready. She found the voluminous photocopy of all the back-and-forth filings in the wrongful death suit. Epstein had submitted a list of property taken: diamond studs, a tennis bracelet, and an engagement ring. The latter was described as an "antique Art Deco ring, a three-carat diamond set in platinum, with a border of diamonds and emeralds, with an estimated value of $20,000." Perhaps he had inflated the cost? She e-mailed the description to her mother and asked if that sounded right to her. Her mother's older brother was a jeweler, he should be able to help.

As she clicked back and forth, she noticed two more look-alikes. Mary Epstein had put on about thirty pounds during her marriage, but she looked eerily like Annette in the earlier photos—tall, thin, blond. Don Epstein had a type. A type that wasn't a far cry from Whitney Talbot. Granted, Whitney's eyes had a fox-like slyness, her jaw was sharper. Whitney's jaw was sharper than most kitchen knives. Still, she was a good match.

Not as Whitney *Talbot*, though. Whitney Talbot was too confident, too rooted. Don Epstein preferred his women a little lost. Like a wolf, he cut the weak ones from the herd. The real Whitney would never appeal to him. But a good cover story could take care of that.

Whitney needed approximately forty seconds to be persuaded.

"I'm in!" she cried happily. "But there's so much *competition.* How do I break through the crowd?"

"I'm not sure," Tess said. "But I think the key is being a little needy. Needy and alone. No family, no friends to speak of."

"So I walk up to him and announce, 'I'm the woman of your dreams—no one will miss me when I'm gone.' "

"We need to stage another damsel-in-distress scenario, like the one you did with Jordan. He was ready to make babies with you after a cup of coffee, remember?"

"He also was a loser. Give Don Epstein credit. He's managed to get away with three or four murders. Don't underestimate him."

"Don't underestimate *me*," Tess said.

Two-fer Tuesday, Whitney thought as she pulled up in front of the check-cashing store in Cherry Hill. She had never been in a check-cashing store. And she only knew the edges of this sad little South Baltimore neighborhood, and that was because it bordered the boathouse from which she and Tess rowed. She had a paper sack of motley dollar bills, which she had spent the last evening crinkling and soiling, so they would look pathetic. She, too, was trying to look pathetic, but fetchingly so. Neither part—pathetic, fetching—came naturally to her. She kept trying to remember to round her shoulders, hang her head.

Once in the store, which Tess had established was the location to which Epstein reported every day, Whitney shoved her bag of money at the cashier and muttered an incoherent string of words. She had wanted to do an accent, but Tess pointed out that she would have to sustain it for hours if she managed to get a date with

Epstein. She had to play stupid instead, and playing stupid was even harder than an accent for Whitney. She tried to remember her newspaper days, how people sometimes managed to get past security and wander into various offices, telling complicated, detailed stories that never quite cohered. She babbled about her mother and her BG&E bill and her car and her cat, the last being completely fictitious. Whatever help was offered, she refused, saying she needed a certified cashier's money order check.

"Which is it?" the cashier asked. "A money order or a cashier's check?"

Whitney accused the woman of being unhelpful, demanded to see the manager. It took about twenty minutes, but the exasperated cashier finally summoned the manager. Another twenty minutes, more faked sobbing and incoherence, until Epstein himself was forced to confront this impossible customer.

"What exactly is the problem?" he asked.

Whitney, much to her own amazement, burst into very real tears. Later, when she tried to figure out why, she couldn't explain it, even to herself. (Actually, she was the only person to whom she attempted to explain this. She would never reveal such a weakness in front of Tess.) But there was something so sad about the man. Sad and wounded.

"I'm Baltimore bred and buttered," Epstein said an hour later, over a round of beers. He had taken her to Nick's, a waterside restaurant along the middle branch of the Patapsco. It was a little chilly this time of year, but the view was grand. And Epstein was surprisingly good company. Why hadn't Tess factored that in? He must have had more than money going for him to land that string of attractive women. He was funny, well-informed about the world, interested in the arts.

But the enchanting thing about Epstein was that he seemed genuinely curious about her. Enchanting, but problematic, as Whitney really hadn't worked that hard on her alternative identity.

"I grew up on the Shore," Whitney said, figuring her two years at Washington College and her parents' summer house in Oxford would allow her to fake that locality. "My dad's a . . . farmer. Sweet corn."

"But you said your mother was a widow, and you were trying to get a money order to pay bills that were on final notice?"

"They're divorced. My mother's second husband just died. That's why I was so upset. He was like a . . . father to me. Even though I have a father, my stepdad and I are very close." She remembered Tess's injunction that Epstein preferred women who were somewhat isolated, lonely. "The weird thing is, my stepdad was the only person to whom I was close. I don't speak to my father at all, and while I'm willing to help my mother out, we don't really have much to do with one another."

"What brought you to Cherry Hill?"

"I just moved to Baltimore this month. Cherry Hill sounded so nice. I thought there would be a hill. With, um, cherries."

"And you don't know who I am?"

"Should I?"

He looked down at the table. "I've been on television a bit, lately."

"I had to hock my television to put a deposit down on my apartment."

"I've been in the newspaper, too."

"I read the Easton *Star-Democrat* when I was still on the Shore, but I haven't been keeping up since I moved here. Why were you in the newspaper?"

Epstein smiled. "It's not important. Another round? Maybe dinner? A girl as thin as you shouldn't go too long between meals."

"I have a freakishly high metabolism," Whitney said. "So maybe we should go to one of those all-you-can-eat buffets, like at Pizza Hut?" Whitney was thin because she was largely indifferent to food. But she would fake her way through a big meal if that's what it took to draw out the evening. She told herself that she was a good friend, doing this for Tess. She tried to ignore the fact that she was having a genuinely good time.

Tess was thinking about dinner, too. Not hers, but the food that Annette Epstein had eaten in the hospital. Could Don Epstein have slipped antibiotics in her food while she was there? And what about the idiopathic nausea that landed her in the hospital but hadn't killed her? She clicked away on the Internet, reading about poison.

Crow walked in, looked over her shoulder and sighed.

"It's fascinating," she said. "It's not that easy to find a poison in someone's system unless you have some idea what it is. Yes, everyone agrees that Annette Epstein had antibiotics in her system. But what about the nausea that put her in the hospital to begin with? Of course they did a tox screen, but that only uncovers so much, and no one was arguing about the cause of Annette's death, which was clearly a complication of the staph infection—"

"Tess, this isn't healthy."

She held up the spiral-bound notepad on the bedside table. "My blood pressure readings have been normal for days."

"I'm talking about your mental health. You set out to get the police's full attention. Mission accomplished. Let it go."

Tess decided this was probably not the best time to tell him that she had sent Whitney out to land a date with Baltimore's best known bachelor. She moved her feet, creating a space for Crow to sit. Of all the things she disliked about her confinement, the worst had been sleeping alone, out here. A small thing, not sleeping in the same bed. No, check that. A big thing, a huge thing. She felt estranged from him. He was loyal, but she realized now she was never truly sure of him. Over the years they had been together, he ran away from her twice. Both times she had all but forced him to leave her, but still—he was the one who ran. What if he ran again?

"Do you remember," she asked, "how we met?"

"I worked in your aunt's bookstore."

"You had a crush on my aunt."

"Everyone who worked in the store had a crush on your aunt. It's a rite of passage."

"When did we fall in love?"

"Isn't that a song from *Fiorello!*?"

"Possibly the worst musical to ever win the Pulitzer, no small feat," Tess said.

"And poor George Gershwin got no recognition when *Of Thee I Sing* won."

The exchange of trivia cheered her. It was normal, it was what they did. "I'm just saying, this all seems so . . . accidental."

"The pregnancy was an accident. Our life together feels purposeful to me. That's why the baby didn't faze me. I always assumed we would have one."

"You did?" It had been a shock, when she first went to see the ob-gyn, to discover the cause of her nausea. The next shock was discovering that she was considered, at thirty-five, an "older" mother. She thought she had all the time in the world to start a family, if that's what she decided she wanted, and then she was told she was a long shot.

"Yes. I just thought I was going to have to launch a campaign. By the way, I know you don't want to make any plans about the baby, but there is one thing we have to talk about."

"Yes?"

"We have to pick out a guardian."

"I thought we settled on Whitney."

"The other day, when I was out with her, I started to ask, but I had second thoughts. I don't think she likes kids, Tess."

"She'll like *our* child."

"She's so . . . rootless. Living in that cottage on her parents' property, working at the family foundation. And she gets bored easily."

Crow had never criticized Whitney before and it made Tess uncomfortable. What else might he criticize? And whom?

"Do you have an alternative in mind?"

"Not really. That bothers me, too. We know a lot of people, but not many intact families, with kids. Soon that's going to be our peer group, that's going to shape how we live. Our life is going to change, Tess."

"I know that."

"Do you?"

This had been a refrain since her pregnancy first became public. *Oh boy, is your life going to change.* Usually, it was said with joy and anticipation. But just as often there was a flicker of malice in it, a misery-loves-company vibe that Tess found disturbing. *No more restaurants,* her friend Jackie, the single mother of a little girl, had pronounced. *That is, no more* real *restaurants. You're not going to see a cloth napkin for another ten, fifteen years.* Others had predicted the end of sleep, sex, travel, reading, a clean house, and clean clothes. Apparently, she and Crow had been having far too much fun and it was now time to pay the piper, to surrender to this invading army of one. Why was this information withheld until it was too late?

"I've heard all the lectures," she told Crow now. "I still think that we can take her to restaurants we like.

And we don't travel that much, so that's not a big deal, and—"

"Tess, I'm talking about your job. A job that, at times, has been dangerous."

"Just the once," she said.

"You were almost killed 'just the once.' And there have been other close calls."

"I'm much more cautious than I used to be."

"That's true," Crow said. "But what about the mundane details? Take, for example, surveillance. What if you're watching someone but I need to go to work and we don't have backup babysitting? Are you going to go on jobs with the baby in the car seat, strap her into a Snugli and go about your day?"

"A baby in a Snugli would be an excellent cover," she said.

"Tess." Crow was as angry and agitated as Tess had ever seen him. "I've never tried to tell you how to conduct your life. But your life isn't strictly yours anymore. I'm not saying you can't continue to work as an investigator. But you could go full-time for an insurance company, or a big law firm."

"What about you, then?" she countered. "Do you think managing a club is a suitable job for a man with a young child? On a typical workday, you head out at five P.M. and come home at four in the morning. You work most of the weekend. What changes are you prepared to make?"

"Fact is, I'm thinking of going back to school, part-time, get one of those weekend MBAs."

Tess almost burst into tears, and for once it wasn't the hormones. Six years ago she had fallen in love with a man who was a musician and an artist, and now he was talking about MBAs?

"No," she said. "That's not you. But what you're talking about—that's not me. An office, working for other people. That's the one thing I can't go back to. Once you've been your own boss, it's impossible to go back."

Her iPhone rang, the jangly tone assigned to Whitney. Crow recognized it, too. After all, he had programmed it.

"Go ahead, take it," he said. "Whatever Nancy Drew and Trixie Belden are cooking up is far more important than the small matter of our future."

Chapter 13

Whitney Talbot had always spoken her mind. Not because she was indifferent to the feelings of others—although, to be honest, that was a big factor—but because it was too much trouble keeping track of lies. Tell the truth and bear the consequences was Whitney's motto. But now she found herself juggling two big lies. She was going on "dates" with Don Epstein, pretending to be a naïve Eastern Shore girl, estranged from her parents and with few financial resources.

And she was lying about those dates to her oldest friend, Tess Monaghan, who had no idea how much she was enjoying her assignment. Don Epstein was surprisingly good company, who suggested almost teenage activities for their evening together. Duckpin bowling, ice skating, even a ceili at a North Baltimore church. Whitney had always thought she would rather drive nails into her eyes then attempt Irish dancing, but Epstein made her feel utterly unself-conscious. Having come into this world exceedingly self-conscious, that was no small thing.

He also was, to use one of her mother's outmoded words, a *gentleman.* True, her mother would be appalled by him, but that would be based on appearances and her mother's idea of status. Don Epstein dressed atrociously, in a style Whitney thought of as Bad Florida. Bright patterned shirts worn untucked, slip-on loafers in sherbety colors. And the jewelry! Epstein wore two large rings, not counting his wedding ring, an ID bracelet, and occasionally a gold chain around his neck. Whitney wondered if there was a polite way to tell him about the etiquette rule that dictated a woman should put on all the jewelry she intends to wear, then remove one piece before leaving the house. Maybe two pieces, in his case.

But she had bigger fish to fry than his wardrobe. She was supposed to get into his house, begin poking around. She had worried, at first, that Epstein would rush their courtship. Now she was worried by its low-key platonic nature. To keep the lie of her identity going, she instructed him to pick her up in the lobby of the Ambassador, an old apartment building on the city's North Side. He returned her there each evening, walking her to the elevator. But he never asked to come up, or tried to kiss her. A relief at first, then a worry. Did he think of her as a sister? Did he not find her attractive?

It took three dates before he began to confide in her. "I hate talking about this," he began, over dinner at Cantler's, a much beloved but out-of-the-way restaurant near Annapolis, the kind of place no one ever found by accident. Epstein preferred out-of-the-way places, Whitney was beginning to notice.

"I admit," she said, "I Googled you."

"I thought you didn't have a computer. That's what you told me, when I asked for your e-mail."

Whitney thought quickly. "There are computers at the library."

"Then you do know."

"I know what's been in the newspaper. I haven't heard your side of it."

He sighed. "I don't want to talk about it now. But next Saturday, there's someplace I'd like to take you. Someplace almost . . . well, sacred to me. Would you do that for me, Whitney? Would you let me take you to this sacred place and explain myself?"

Of course she would.

Tess was happy to know that Whitney was spending so much time with Don Epstein, although it didn't seem that she was learning very much. "Pin him down," she reminded Whitney the next time they spoke on the phone. "Get him to talk about Carole, take you to the house. You're looking for inconsistencies, remember, the sort of details that reveal a lie."

"I have to say, he's been remarkably consistent. He's very melancholy, in a way."

Tess snorted. " 'Melancholy' is an interesting choice of word."

"Well, if he's a liar—"

"If?"

"He's a remarkably good one."

"Sociopaths usually are," Tess said. She felt a prickle of worry. "On this next date, Whitney? The one where he's taking you someplace special?"

"Sacred," Whitney corrected.

"Whatever. Be . . . careful. It wouldn't be a bad idea to take a handgun in your purse. I know you have rifles and shotguns, but you still have a handgun as well, right?"

"Tess, there's no reason he would want to hurt me. I don't know anything. If you're right, he kills for financial gain, to trade in one model for the next, and the previous model is indisputably gone."

"Or he kills because someone knows too much. I think that was the case with Carole. She found something, maybe his second wife's engagement ring, which he claimed was stolen."

"You know, that doesn't prove he killed her—"

"Whitney, whose side are you on?"

"I'm just trying to keep you tethered to the facts."

Tess wished she could see her old friend's face, but she stopped by less and less these days, preferring to check in by telephone.

"Here are some facts, Whitney, in case you've forgotten. Three dead women. One missing, *at best.* Be careful."

"Okay, okay."

Tess's computer beeped, announcing the arrival of an e-mail. She had once loathed e-mail, but now it was her lifeline. She even found herself IM'ing at times. This one was from her mother, who had attached a file. Tess didn't even know her mother knew how to attach files.

Isn't this the ring you asked me to research? she had written. *I was trying to find out how common the design was, and my search terms yielded this item on eBay. Looks awfully similar to me.*

Interesting indeed. Far more interesting to Tess was the seller's location, listed as Glen Burnie, a mere few miles south of Cherry Hill. Could Epstein be that stupid? She clicked on *Other items by this seller* and found a pair of diamond earrings, a tennis bracelet, and several other items—bracelets, pins, necklaces. Except for the ring, it was what she considered mallish—expensive, but not distinctive. Diamond studs and a tennis bracelet had been listed among Annette Epstein's missing effects. Did the other pieces belong to her as well? How to explain the ID bracelet with "DM" on it? Did it stand for Don and Mary? Or Danielle Massinger?

He gave Danielle a lot of jewelry, Mrs. Zimmerman had said. *Gave it—and took it back after pushing her down the stairs?* This could be what Carole Epstein had found, which was why she had to disappear. Annette's jewelry proved only that Epstein was a liar and a fraud. Danielle's jewelry proved he could never let go of anything.

Tess clicked *Ask the seller a question,* using her personal account, TEMonaghan@aol.com. She was interested in the ID bracelet, she wrote, but had been burned in other online auctions. Could the seller provide any details about its provenance?

Three days later Whitney couldn't help remembering Tess's warning as Don Epstein drove farther and farther into the country, racing the sunset. "We should have gotten an earlier start," he said. "We'll never make it before dark. But I have some flashlights."

Flashlights? She knew he liked out of the way places, but this was ridiculous. She didn't feel so silly now, slipping her handgun into her purse. He turned on a roughly paved road, then a gravel one, then a dirt lane. She had mocked Tess's iPhone, but it had a GPS function, something she would dearly love to have right now. Where was she? Somewhere in Carroll County, north of Union Mills. The last street sign she had noticed was Humbert School House Road, a nice Nabokovian touch in the middle of nowhere. She had tried to call Epstein's attention to it, but he didn't know the reference and didn't find it funny when she explained it.

"Child molesters," he said, "should be killed. I was disappointed when the Supreme Court struck down the death penalty for rape." It was the first little splinter of dissatisfaction she had experienced in his company. *A man who believed in the death penalty—ugh.* Then: *Does he believe in applying it on his own?*

"Are we there yet?" she asked, trying for a joking tone.

"Almost," he said.

"You know, this has the feel of a horror film. Two people, out in the middle of the country on a dark night."

"Not a horror film," Don Epstein said. "This is a love story. A very sad one."

Tess checked her e-mail for perhaps the quadrillionth time. The eBay seller never replied, and now the items had been removed. *Stupid, stupid, stupid.* She should have bid on one of the cheaper items, seen what information could be gleaned. Somehow, she had alerted Epstein that she was on to him—and now he was out with Whitney. How had he made the connection? He didn't know her name. Shoot—the photograph with Dempsey, the one used on the *Today* show. If he had plugged "Monaghan" into an image search . . . *Stupid, stupid, stupid.*

She had thought such mistakes were behind her. Her learning curve as a private detective had been a steep one, but it was a long time since she'd done something truly boneheaded. She loved her job. True, she hadn't dreamed about being a private investigator when she was a child. What child ever did? But once she found this vocation, she realized she was made for it. Much as she had realized she was made for Crow once she found him. Now it seemed she must choose between the two.

She had meant what she told Crow. The one thing she could never do was work for someone else again. Except—*never* was a big word. If it came down to putting food on the table, one would do just about anything. And Crow had already compromised quite a bit, shelving his own dreams. What was she going to do? What were they going to do? Stymied, she refreshed the eBay page. Empty.

Don Epstein stopped near a small wire fence, thick with rust. "I bought the land twenty years ago, thinking to build a house out here for Mary and me. Then I found out about *this*."

"A garden?"

"An old cemetery. All my wives are buried here."

"All?" Whitney's voice squeaked a little. "I mean, um, both?"

"Mary and Annette. It's not exactly legal to do that, you know, so please don't tell anyone. They didn't have anyone but me, so I didn't think it mattered."

So there was a body to be exhumed, Whitney thought. Tess would be thrilled.

"Only one other person even knows about this place, and that was Carole." He seemed on the verge of tearing up. "I'm sorry now, but you see—it started with Annette."

Oh dear. What, exactly, had started with Annette? Thank God she had her handgun in her purse. Which was in the car. *Damn, damn, damn.*

"I met Annette at a meeting for people who were grieving. Carole was the one who persuaded me to go. Annette had lost her husband to cancer. We started dating. And when I decided to marry her, I brought her out here and asked her, right here, at Mary's grave site. You know Mary was my high school sweetheart, right?"

Whitney nodded. God, her throat was suddenly so dry, her lips almost stuck together. Perhaps she could ask to get her purse, in order to apply some Carmex?

"I admit, I never loved Annette quite as much as I loved Mary. Annette was great. Sweet, considerate. I couldn't believe it when she got sick. And when she died . . . But you know what they say: A hospital is no place to be ill. So she was gone and there was Carole . . . I had no options, Whitney. None."

Whitney realized that Epstein, while declaring his love for these women, had not declared his innocence in their deaths. The two things would seem contradictory to most people, of course. But was Epstein most people? Had he managed to blank out his responsibility for his wives' deaths? Was that why he was such a persuasive tragic figure, one on one, because he no longer remembered that he had caused his own bereavement?

"Whitney, Whitney, Whitney," he said. "I have brought you here today because I know you are not the woman you claim to be."

She should really get her purse. "I should really get my purse."

He shook his head. "Take my hand, Whitney."

She did, realizing that it was the first time they had touched in any intimate way. As recently as a day ago she would have been at least curious about physical contact with Epstein. Now she wanted to snatch her hand and run. But where would she go?

"Whitney, you are not alone in this world. You are not without resources."

Oh, dear. "I really need my purse."

Don Epstein shook his head, placing his hands between hers, kneeling before her.

"Kneel with me, Whitney."

"The ground looks awfully damp—" He jerked her down the ground.

"Pray with me, Whitney. Absolve me, Whitney. I feel I can tell you the truth. I am responsible for Mary's death."

"Oh, I can understand why you would feel that way—"

"No, Whitney. I killed her as surely as if I pulled that trigger myself. Will you pray with me, Whitney?"

"Um, sure."

Tess, dozing, was awaked by her daughter's nightly gymnastic routine and a comfortably familiar hollow feeling in her stomach. Who was supposed to be bringing dinner tonight? Lloyd? Mrs. Blossom? She had forgotten to ask Crow when he left for work. How late was it? Late enough that when she opened Dempsey's crate, the dog insisted on relieving himself in the chamber pot. Great.

Finally, there was a discreet knock, then the door opened, a sharp rat-a-tat of high heels on the wooden floors. Ah, that would be Mrs. Blossom. No, her mother, because Mrs. Blossom never wore heels. Esskay and Miata, shut up in the bedroom, scratched and whined, then settled back down. Would it be Afghan food? Tess recalled telling Crow that morning that she craved *kaddo borawni*, the Helmand's pumpkin appetizer. She sighed in happy anticipation.

"Mom?" she called out.

"No," said the woman in the green raincoat.

In her hand she held what would appear to be a black and violet flashlight to the untrained eye. But Tess's eye happened to be trained by the endless stream of catalogs she received at her office. It was a taser, a small one. But even the small ones had ranges of up to twenty-five feet.

"What's the matter, Carole?" she said. "Couldn't you find one in green?"

Chapter 14

So you're alive," Tess said.

"Yes, and trying to make a new life for myself."

The woman in the green raincoat, seen up close, was as pretty and girlish as Tess's first impression of her. Too girlish, little girlish, all but stomping her foot in frustration.

"You were the eBay seller." She watched as Carole moved briskly around the room, lowering the shades. Cautious, but unnecessary. There were no lights on the houses to either side of Tess's, no one around to see or hear what was about to happen. What was about to happen? "Not Don, but you. You have Annette's jewelry. You have your sister's jewelry. Which means—"

"Which means what, exactly? I took the items down. There's no record anymore."

"I cached them," Tess lied.

"Really?" Carole Epstein looked mildly impressed. Then she picked up Tess's laptop from her cluttered bedside table, held it high above her head and dropped it to the floor. In his crate, Dempsey yipped, but tentatively.

"Shut up," Carole said.

Tess considered her options. No matter the taser's range, Carole wasn't going to settle for stunning her. She meant to kill her, and would press it against her neck again and again until the job was done.

"It won't look like a heart attack," she told Carole. "There will be bruising, maybe even a burn mark. You won't fool a good medical examiner."

"Who cares? You're the one who's been harp, harp, harping that I'm the victim of foul play. People will think the real killer did you in because you wouldn't shut up."

"But they won't blame Don Epstein. I happen to know he has a pretty good alibi for tonight."

"Really?"

"He's on a date."

Carole paced, glancing at the items in Tess's room. "I'll turn over some furniture, take a few things, make it look like a robbery. I'll be in Mozambique long before anyone thinks to look for me."

"Mozambique?"

"It's a good place to disappear," Carole said. "If you have enough money. No extradition treaty with the U.S. And Don was pretty generous when I told him I wanted out. True, he didn't know that I was taking even more than he agreed to give me, but Don was always generous, except when Annette got her hooks into him. Oh, the sweet little widow. She wasn't so grief-struck that she didn't do her best to get Don to cut me off, which was *not* part of the plan."

"You killed Annette."

"I would have, if the staph infection hadn't beat me to it. She had a sweet tooth, so I started bringing her muffins loaded with antibiotics." *She wanted to start a gift-basket business,* Mrs. Zimmerman had said. *She made a good muffin.* "I was going to give her a potassium spike while she was in the hospital, but I didn't have to. I'm lucky that way."

"Lucky?"

"I get what I want, just by thinking about it. When I was thirteen, I got in a big fight with my mother. I wanted to buy a designer skirt and she said I couldn't use my savings. My own savings. I screamed at her, I said, 'I wish you were dead.' Two days later, she was. After that, I always knew I was special, that I could get whatever I wanted."

"And you wanted Don Epstein?"

Carole made a face. "Don't be silly. I wanted him to marry my sister." She looked at the taser. "I think this would be less painful. If I go with the burglary scenario, I'll have to use a kitchen knife."

Tess had a feeling that Carole was more concerned about what blood would do to her coat than about easing Tess mercifully into the next world. The thing was to stall, to try to stay alive until her dinner arrived.

"The burglary is too much like the carjacking," she said. "And you've always been so careful not to repeat yourself, Carole."

As a little girl Whitney had owned a music box, which played a song that began "In the gloaming, oh my darling." What was a gloaming? Was it a place or a quality of light? She remembered only that the trees were sobbing there. And now Don Epstein, cradling her hands in a grip that she couldn't imagine breaking, was sobbing.

"It's not uncommon," she said, "to blame oneself. But it was just bum luck. Right? You stopped for someone in distress—"

"No," he choked out, "no. It was my fault because I didn't take her seriously. But who would? Who would think that an eighteen-year-old girl would do such a thing? Yes, I told her that I wanted to marry Danielle, but that I couldn't afford to divorce Mary. Her father willed the stores to her, so they weren't marital property under Maryland law. But I never expected . . . I never intended . . ."

It took Whitney a second to remember just who Danielle was. But once she did, she had no trouble filling in the missing bits of Epstein's disjointed tale.

"But you didn't tell police who shot you and Mary. That made you an accomplice."

"They were treating me like a suspect the moment I came out of surgery. Who would ever believe that I didn't ask her to do it? She told me she'd cut a deal, hang me out to dry. So we reached an agreement. I'd marry Danielle, take care of both of them. And even when Danielle died, I did what I could for her . . . for a while."

Tess knew Carole wasn't stupid. The woman recognized that she was stalling, if not the reason why. Carole was advancing on her, taser drawn, when Tess's iPhone rang. "Para Donde Vas," the ring tone Crow had assigned to himself.

"It's my boyfriend," Tess said. "He'll panic if I don't answer because he knows exactly where I am."

Carole nodded, standing over her. "Short answers," she hissed.

"Is Lloyd there?" Crow asked. "It's been two hours since he borrowed my car for the dinner run."

"No," Tess said.

"He probably stopped to see May and lost track of time. You know how he is when he gets access to a car. It brings out the teenager in him. Which is only fair, given that he's eighteen."

"Yes."

"Tess, are you mad at me still? I'm sorry that I said I didn't think Whitney would be a good guardian. And the job thing—well, we'll find a solution. Don't be angry, Tess. You're not still, are you?"

"No," she all but choked out. "God, no. I love you, Crow."

"Love you, too. Don't be too hard on Lloyd when he shows up." He clicked off.

"Love," Carole said with disdain. "What a waste."

"Why did you marry Don Epstein, then?"

"For the spousal immunity. Sort of like the Cold War, you know? Neither one of us could strike first. He was weak. I needed something to hold over him."

"Does he know about Annette?"

"You mean that she was a bloodsucking gold digger? Neither one of us saw that coming. I picked her out, in fact. Don's one of those men who needs a companion. I never expected her to put the squeeze on Don, to demand that he cut off his monthly payments to me. Once she was gone, I knew I couldn't make that mistake again. I'd have to marry Don if I wanted his money. It was a business deal."

"And why did you decide to end your lovely business arrangement?"

Carole tossed her head. It was all too easy to imagine her at thirteen, throwing a fit over a Dolce & Gabbana skirt. It was harder to see her as an adult, holding down a job, meeting anyone's expectations but her own.

"Let me guess: He figured out that you killed Danielle. *He* found her jewelry and Annette's among your things, and he was repulsed, maybe even terrified. So you struck a deal. You would disappear in such a way that no one could be really sure what happened—and you wouldn't come back, as long as Don kept the money flowing into those private accounts you set up. Your own sister. Jesus, *I'm* repulsed."

"She was going to tell the police about the affair, how she suspected Don set up the carjacking. She called me at school, in the middle of the week, and I came home late that night to talk to her. I didn't mean to—I just tried to grab her arm at the top of the stairs and . . . well, Dani's balance was never very good."

"It's interesting," Tess said, "how many accidents happen around you. And how careful you are to avoid implicating yourself in anything by Mary Epstein's death, which you can always blame on Epstein."

"You know what?" Carole said. "I'll happily take responsibility for yours, you buttinsky bitch."

The gloaming—it was the last light of day, Whitney finally remembered, not a place—had come and gone. It was pitch-black, the kind of darkness to which the eyes never really adjust. She wasn't sure she believed a word that Don Epstein had told her, but that didn't seem to be the best tack.

Instead she asked: "Why are you confiding in me, Don?"

"Isn't it obvious? I'm in love with you. But I can never divorce Carole, she won't allow it. And if I go down to the police station and make a clean breast of things, they'll lock me up. I want to be with you, Whitney. But I'll never be able to marry you."

Whitney fought down the impulse to scream *Thank God!* Instead, she pulled her hand, ever so gently, from Epstein's grasp and patted his cheek.

"But we can be engaged," she said. "In a matter of speaking. We can live together, as husband and wife, after a decent interval has passed. No one needs to know that you haven't legally severed your ties to Carole."

"You would do that?"

"Yes. Now—Now let's go tell my mom the happy news."

"Doesn't she live in Easton? Aren't you estranged?"

"Um, not anymore."

One look at you and she'll make stiff drinks for all of us. She also would insist on giving Epstein a tour of the house, Whitney thought, which would allow her to call the police. She wanted to skip back to the car. She couldn't help being pleased with herself. Tess was never going to believe what had really happened. Plus a proposal, to boot, her very first. Of course, it wasn't really for her, but the girl she had pretended to be these last two weeks. Still, it was something.

Tess knew she probably wouldn't die at the taser's first contact, but she would be immobilized. *More* immobilized. She could try to heave herself out of bed, but she couldn't outrun a snail in her condition. Instead, as Carole approached, she picked up the cane her aunt had given her and tried to push the panic button on the alarm console above her head. But the angle was awkward, and Carole knocked the cane away, although not out of Tess's grip. She was thrown a little off-balance, her high heels catching on the rug. In that split-second, Tess used the cane as she had used it so many times, to open the door on Dempsey's crate.

Freed, the dog rushed toward his former mistress—going straight for the hem of her coat, trying to shred it with his teeth. Carole screamed and kicked at the dog, but he was quite the little sidewinder, evading her every move. Carole tried to use her weapon on him, but Tess rapped her right wrist sharply with the cane and the taser fell, skittering across the floor. Carole crawled after it, the dog nipping at her legs and backside. But now Carole was out of cane range, her hands closing over the taser, and she might fire it from there in her desperation.

Searching frantically for something, anything, she could reach from the bed, Tess risked leaning forward and hefting the chamber pot, throwing its contents at Carole Epstein's face. Shocked, Carole let go of the taser with an outraged screech, but Tess wasn't through. She managed to heave the chamber pot at the woman's head, hitting her midsection instead. This gave Tess the time she needed to grab the cane and hit the panic button, sounding a wail of an alarm that could be heard up and down the street. Dempsey continued to bite and tear, as if intent on shredding that raincoat. This was the battle for which he had been preparing, this was his enemy, the coldhearted mistress who had staged her disappearance and left him behind.

Tess felt a sharp pain in her midsection, quite unlike anything she had ever known. Had she torn something, or—worse? The pain shot through her again and she looked for her phone, which had been knocked from the table in the struggle. Scooping it up, she called 911, screaming her address into the phone, asking for an ambulance, even as the house phone rang, probably the alarm company. Good, they would call police if she didn't pick up and provide the code.

Carole Epstein was up on her feet again, now intent only on getting away, but Lloyd, truly better late than never, picked that moment to arrive with Tess's dinner. Bless street-smart Lloyd, he didn't need to be told that a woman dripping with dog urine was someone who should be detained. Tess could hear them scuffling, and the whole neighborhood probably could hear Carole Epstein's ugly screams and epithets.

"Release the hounds," Tess cried to Lloyd, and he ran to the bedroom to let out Esskay and Miata, who had been scratching at the door all the while. For the first time, the three dogs worked in concert together, their fealty to Tess overriding their previous disputes.

"They've got her cornered in the dining room," Lloyd said breathlessly, crouching by her. "Who is that crazy lady? Did she hurt you?"

"I don't know, Lloyd. I called 911—something—it feels—I need to get to the hospital, but you have to stay here with her until the police can take her away. Tell the police that she assaulted me, that she's a killer, and not to let her go under any circumstances. Then call the club and get Crow on the phone, tell him to meet me at Hopkins."

"Tess—is the baby coming?"

"Maybe. I don't know. I don't know what's going on inside me."

In Baltimore public schools, they tell you in sixth grade where babies come from, but precocious Tess Monaghan had scored that information from her older cousins before she was eight. Now, at thirty-five, in despair over her lack of maternal instincts, she had finally learned where mothers come from. She knew what it was like to fight for her own life, but this had been different. She was defending her daughter. Now she could only hope that she hadn't killed her in the process.

Chapter 15

No one should long to forget the night her first child is born, but Tess Monaghan did. She wished she could erase every detail of the evening from her mind. Not just that evening, but the weeks that followed as well. Upon arrival at Johns Hopkins, she was taken to an operating room for an emergency C-section. She begged them to wait for Crow, but there was no time to spare. She and her daughter were both in distress. "Your husband wouldn't be allowed in the O.R., anyway," a nurse told her, meaning to console her.

Yes, take the baby away from me, Tess thought as she slipped under the anesthesia. *Save her from me.* The adrenaline of the encounter with Carole Epstein had ebbed and Tess no longer saw herself as her child's warrior-mother, but her greatest liability. Oh, hadn't she been clever, sitting there with her iPhone and her laptop and her composition books. The Land of Counterpane indeed, fighting her battles with toys and proxies. Then one of the toy soldiers had shown up, larger and far more lethal than she seemed at a distance. *I wouldn't be surprised if a Department of Social Services worker is waiting when I wake up, ready to take the baby from me.*

Instead, there was Crow.

"She's fine," he said quickly. "In neonatal intensive care because she's only thirty-four weeks. But she's almost four pounds, which is pretty good."

"What does she look like?"

"My hair, your eyes, and a little rosebud of a mouth that's wholly her own. She doesn't look like a Fifi, though. We need a real name."

But Tess had always known the name she wanted. She just hadn't allowed herself to say it out loud. "The tradition is to pick someone who's died. Remember my friend Carl? I'd like to name her Carla."

Crow hesitated, and Tess thought he might object, that he might want a less sad legacy for their daughter. Carl had died under such horrible circumstances. But wasn't all death horrible? "I'll agree to Carla if you let me have the middle name I want: Scout."

Tess smiled. "Carla Scout Monaghan. It will make my mother *insane*!" Then she realized that she was a mother herself, and the thought of making a parent insane had suddenly lost much of its appeal.

It turned out that Carla Scout was years away from such empathetic insight. Two days later she had a hemorrhage, apparently just for the hell of it.

The neonatal intensive care unit was pretty much the saddest place that Tess Monaghan had ever known, and she had seen her share of sad places. All those tiny babies, all those devastated parents. Carla Scout was the biggest patient, a behemoth. "Why is she even here?" Tess overheard one mother whisper the first week. She knew from the nurses that this woman's son had been born at twenty-six weeks, so tiny that he could fit in the palm of one's hand. Carla Scout Monaghan was huge by comparison. Yes, *looking* at her, even in the Isolette, in that welter of tubes and machines, it was hard to see that anything was wrong. Tess wanted to lean over and hiss: "She had a hemorrhage. We're waiting to see how this will affect her. Happy now?"

Yet she knew the other mother was simply trying to find a place to offload her fear and terror. Tess couldn't blame her. She wanted to do the same thing. Problem was, her anger and fear always circled back to her.

She had to blame herself. No one else would. She wished Crow would throw it in her face, how he had told her that her obsession with the Epsteins was unhealthy. She recalled how Mrs. Zimmerman warned her that morbid thoughts would warp her baby. She remembered Lenhardt telling her that parenthood would be her greatest joy, and if she were unlucky, her greatest sorrow. Yes, all the fairies had come to her child's christening. But she was the one who had cursed her.

"If only—" she began one afternoon.

"Stop, Tess," Crow said, taking her hand. This time she listened. She was sitting in one of the rocking chairs placed among the Isolettes. Carla Scout had been here almost a month. Halloween, Thanksgiving, her official due date had come and gone. Tess's stitches had dissolved, she had pumped gallons of breast milk, hoping she might one day feed her own child. But for now the baby lived in this Isolette. Back home, the leaves had fallen and Stony Run Park was so stark and bare that Tess could see through to the other side—all the way to Blythewood Road. Blythewood. Blithe Wood. A pretty name for a pretty street where two exceedingly ugly people had lived. But she had been the blithe one, thinking she controlled everything.

Spouses can't be compelled to testify, but there's no law against *volunteering* to do so, and the Epsteins proved quite eager to trade allegations. *She* killed Mary Epstein. *He* kept two sets of books, bilked his own company, and killed Danielle when she found out. *She* stole her sister's jewelry and Annette's, too. No, *he's* the one who had the jewelry all along. Tess wished there were a system in which the two of them could be locked up forever, with only each other's company. *That* would be justice. Instead, Don pleaded to twenty years, while Carole was holding out for a trial in Mary Epstein's death. It couldn't be proved that she pushed her sister down the stairs, and even if she had sickened Annette with antibiotic-laden muffins, they weren't the cause of her death. Frankly, Tess thought someone should go back and look at the car accident that had taken the lives of Carole's parents. She wouldn't put anything past the woman.

But she had no room in her head for the Epsteins, not anymore. Everything was the baby—the sad, silent journey back and forth to Hopkins, the empty evenings, the spike of fear every time a phone rang. She let her father work on the nursery because it was clearly *his* way of coping, but it depressed her, watching the room take shape. The days dragged by. Some families triumphed and took their children home. New families arrived to take their place. And some families—well, some families, she just didn't want to think about.

"I've seen much sicker babies than yours get better," the nurse told Tess. The nurses were goddesses in NICU, the ones the parents trusted. Tess asked them again and again: "Did I do this to my baby?" They always said no. She wanted to believe them.

After the hemorrhage, the doctors had hustled Tess and Crow into a place the parents called the Room. The Room was like something out of a Stephen King novel, a perfectly bland conference room where the most horrible things happened. Unearthly sounds, inhuman sounds, emanated from the Room. The day they took Tess and Crow to the Room, the doctors were quite gentle. No, it wasn't good that she had hemorrhaged. But it was only a two on a four-point scale. They had seen babies suffer much worse and go on to lead full and normal lives.

"Did I do this to my baby?" Tess asked.

The doctor said no, that her premature labor was a godsend. Her placenta had failed, something absolutely outside her control, the baby had stopped getting nourishment. An emergency C-section would have been ordered after Tess's next ultrasound. She didn't believe him.

Christmas zipped by, then New Year's, squares on a calendar. Tess's laptop was restored to life, but she seldom turned it on.

On the first Monday in January, she and Crow showed up at the hospital—and were taken to the Room again. She reached for Crow's hand; it was slick with sweat.

"I want to tell you," their doctor said, "that I think Carla Scout is ready to go home. You'll need oxygen and a monitor—"

"She's going home?" Tess asked. "Just like that?" She didn't know it was possible to get good news in the Room. She didn't trust it.

"We're pretty good at what we do here," the doctor said. "Think of it this way. She was six weeks early. She's going home only a few weeks after her original due date."

"But how—I mean, what do you know? How can you be sure? What about her vision? What about brain development? Respiratory problems?" Tess cast around, trying to remember all the other dire things she had read on the Internet. "Are you *sure* she's okay?"

"Carla Scout is stable. She has no impairment that we can detect. But no, Tess, I don't have a crystal ball. You want me to give you some kind of guarantee that everything will be fine, forever. I can't do that. I can't do that for any of our patients. Oh, I'm reasonably sure that your daughter has no lingering effects from the premature delivery. However, you and Crow—you and

Crow most certainly do. And you're going to have to get over it. Welcome to parenthood."

They left the NICU, stunned with happiness. Tess realized that her hair was dirty and her clothes didn't feel quite clean. When had she last bathed? Back when she was on bed rest she had promised herself that she would shower once, twice, three times a day when her confinement had passed. She had planned to exercise every day and indulge in wine again. Now she was thin, yet flabby, and couldn't remember if she had even bothered to have a glass of champagne on New Year's Eve five days ago. Almost certainly not. Five days ago she had nothing to toast. Now she wanted to sing, skip through the busy hive that was Hopkins Hospital. Her daughter was coming home. She was going to get a chance to screw her up in all the normal ways.

"I guess we can get married now," Crow said. "And finally have the baby shower that you kept vetoing."

"Oh, right," Tess said. She knew they had forgotten something. How funny to think she had once been obsessed about getting a ring from Crow. She had worried that he would skip out on her, that he wouldn't be there if things got tough. Well, that was one worry gone. He had been a rock these past two months. She thought of the moment when Carole had stood over her and she told Crow she loved him, thinking she might never speak to him again. They were going to get married. They would fight. They would argue. They would be irritated with one another. That was how marriage worked. Except, possibly, for Mrs. Blossom. But Tess hoped she never forgot what it felt like to speak to him that night, Crow's casual, "Love you, too."

"You know," she said now, her voice taking on a teasing tone that felt rusty and strange in her mouth. There had not been much teasing as of late. "You know, I didn't think you were going to ask me to marry you. After all, you told Lloyd he could have the family heirloom."

"*One* of the family heirlooms," Crow said. "I held the better one back for you. You always forget—my family used to be well-to-do, Tess."

"Used to be," she said. "Now you're poor like me."

"Funny," he said, "I feel pretty rich right now."

They went for breakfast at a beloved restaurant, the Golden West, and ate their way across the world—sopapillas, pancakes, French toast, poached eggs in green curry, limeaide, and layer cake. *We'll bring Carla Scout here*, Tess thought. *We'll take her everywhere. We won't treat her as if she's made out of glass. She's sturdy, like her mother.*

The combination wedding/baby shower was over, but some guests lingered. May could not get enough of Carla Scout. Tess thought this would scare her two mommies, but Liz explained it was a hardwired instinct, this love of infants, essential to their survival. "I heard it on NPR." Tess's parents were in the kitchen, washing up in a silence that she now knew was companionable, the soft embers of a romance kindled by her mother's fastidious consumption of popcorn. Crow's mother was admiring the sweaters and caps made by Mrs. Blossom; apparently, an older woman sitting on a bench, knitting, was the greatest cover ever in surveillance. Mrs. Blossom had broken three cases of insurance fraud since January and could barely keep up with all the requests for her services, now that Valentine's Day was near.

But it was Whitney who outlasted all the other guests, cataloging the gifts that people had brought in defiance of Tess's instructions.

"Just think," she said, "it could have been a double ceremony."

"You never told me," Tess said, "how Epstein reacted when you brought him to your mother's house and explained that you weren't exactly who he thought you were."

"He was a pretty good sport," Whitney said. "You know what? I think the pump was primed. He was terrified of Carole. It was probably only a matter of time before she killed him. Someone named Harold

Lenhardt has sent you a very pretty dress. Well, not you, but Carla Scout. I can't see you squeezing into this frock." She held up a summery dress.

"Carla Scout will swim in that. She's still just at fiftieth percentile for height." Strange, they had never planned to use both names, but it suited the baby somehow, who had lost much of her hair and developed a skeptical squint in her still-hazel eyes. Lord, how she would hate them some day, for saddling her with that unwieldy name. Much as she had once hated her parents for making her Theresa Esther. Could have been worse. She could have been Shirley.

"And this is from me." Whitney handed Tess a flat box. It was a baby book, a pink and white one without a shred of irony. "There's a place for the first lock of hair, and all the developmental milestones." Tess's heart lurched a little. *The doctor had said—no, settle down.* "But the best part is this page, where you write down the story of her birthday. And who has a better one than you?"

"Whitney—"

"Come on, all's well that ends well. You don't have to put in the part about the dog urine, or the taser. But you have to give Dempsey his due. Dempsey loves Carla Scout."

This was true. Tess suspected the dog, now relegated to being one of the pack, was relieved that someone smaller was finally on the premises.

"I don't think one page could ever be enough," Tess said. "Where do I start? With the discovery I was pregnant? The day I met Crow?"

"You better write small, if you're going back that far," Whitney said. "Just don't leave out my part. I'm the comic relief."

Tess picked up a pen, but instead of marring the pristine baby book, she grabbed one of the black-and-white composition books she always had close at hand.

"Dear Carla Scout," she began. *"In the weeks that I was waiting for you, I had to stay in bed, where I spent most of my time staring out the window. One day, I saw a girl in a green raincoat . . ."*

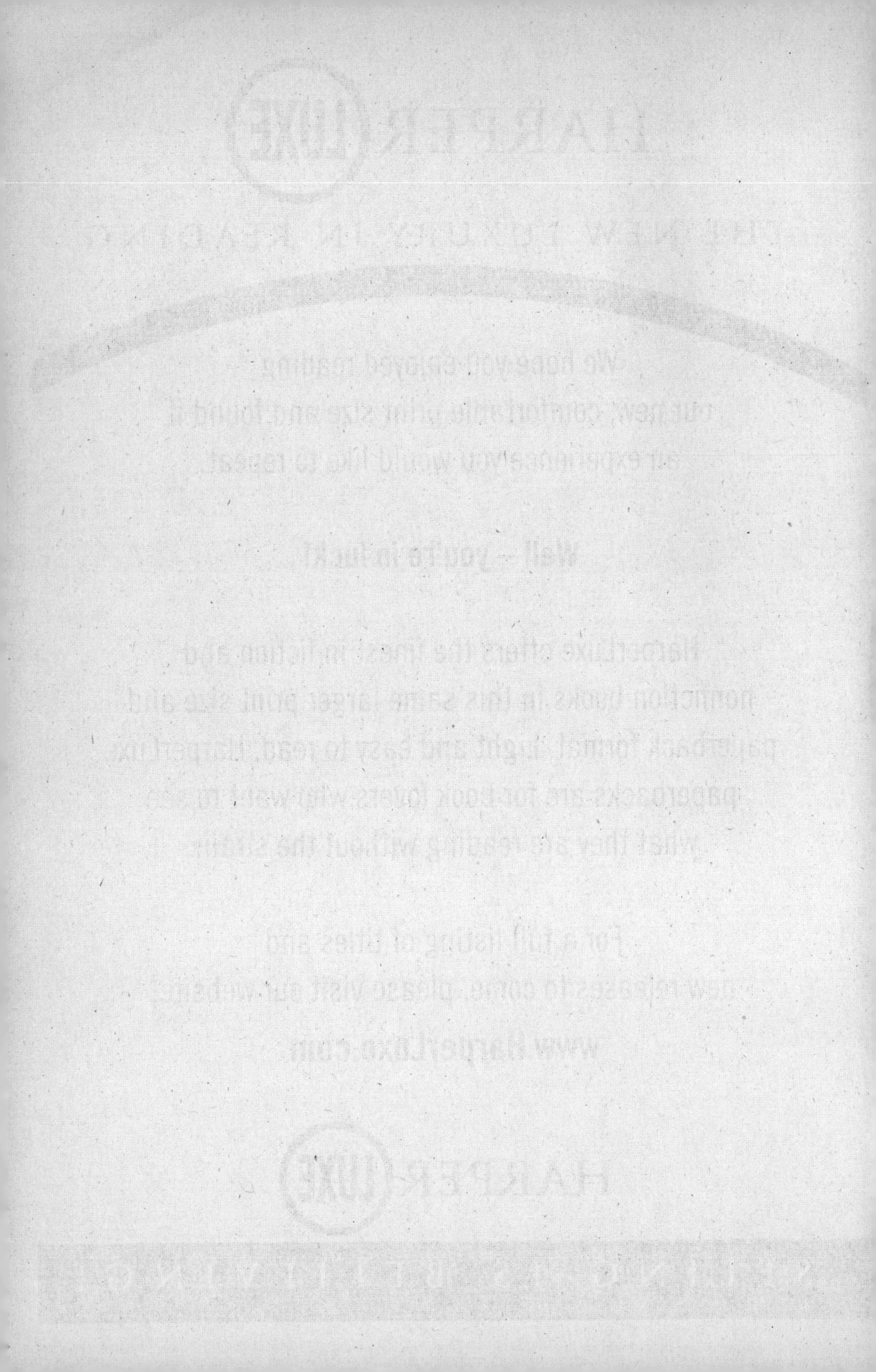